JUDEX

The Black Coat Script Library

1. Randy & Jean-Marc Lofficier – *Despair* (based on a novel by Marc Agapit; illustrations by Sylvain Despretz)
2. Mike Baron – *The Iron Triangle*
3. Emma Bull & Will Shetterly – *War for the Oaks* (based on a novel by Emma Bull)
4. Steve Englehart – *Majorca*
5. Emma Bull & Will Shetterly – *Nightspeeder* (illustrations by Kevin O'Neill)
6. Andrew Paquette – *Peripheral Vision*
7. James D. Hudnall – *Devastator* (based on his comic book)
8. Randy & Jean-Marc Lofficier – *Royal Flush*
9. Gerry Conway & Roy Thomas – *Doc Dynamo*
10. Roy Thomas & Janis Hendler – *Rivers of Time* (based on a novel by L. Sprague de Camp)
11. Randy & Jean-Marc Lofficier – *City* (inspired by a novel from Joël Houssin)

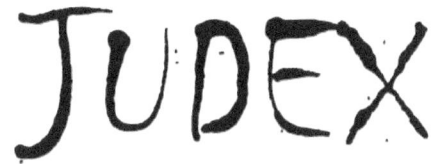

JUDEX

screenplay by
Robert L. Robinson, Jr.

inspired by the character created by
Arthur Bernède & Louis Feuillade

Foreword by
Bill Mechanic

A Black Coat Press Book

Screenplay & introduction © 2012 by Robert L. Robinson, Jr.
Foreword © 2012 by Bill Mechanic.
Cover art Copyright © 2012 by John Pinkerton.

Also available from Black Coat Press:
Judex (the original novel by Arthur Bernède & Louis Feuillade, translated by Rick Lai) ISBN 9781612270852
Belphégor (a novel by Arthur Bernède, translated by Jean-Marc & Randy Lofficier), ISBN 9781612271101

Forthcoming:
The Shadow of Judex, a collection of Judex stories including Robert L. Robinson's "The Two Hunters."

Visit our website at www.blackcoatpress.com

Foreword

I am hardly an expert on *Judex*, but I not only have seen two of the three versions, I have a rare poster of Louis Feuillade's 1913 release prominently displayed in my house. I first saw George Franju's version when I was in film school and, being a comic book fan, thought it inescapable that this French film hero pre-dated and greatly informed the later American comic book and film heroes, not the least of which is Batman. While not a great fan of most remakes, I thought *Judex* was prime for a Hollywood entry.

I never followed up on that instinct, but a few years ago, Robert Robinson contacted me about doing another film version of a comic book, *DeadWorld*, which we're presently hoping to get up on the screen next year. While discussing *DeadWorld*, Robinson asked if I would read a script he'd written. Sure, what is it? Well, he said, it's an English language version of a great French film character—Judex.

That script is now being published. Hopefully, someone will read and want to make it into a film. While Judex is undoubtedly revered in France, this is a character the rest of the world should get to know.

Bill Mechanic
Chief Executive Officer,
Pandemonium Films

Introduction
Judex and Me

Judex began for me outside Philadelphia in 2004 in a place named King of Prussia, Pennsylvania. Many people, both locals and visitors to its massive mall which is its primary claim to fame, believe the area was named for Fredrick II also referred to as Fredrick the Great, but that's not true. It's actually named after a tavern, The King of Prussia Inn, which was in reality named for good ol' Freddy. To get an entire region named for a bar is either a tribute to the bartender or the bar maid. I'm betting on the bartender. A good bar maid can bring you in, but a great bartender keeps you coming back.

From outside our windows of the office, in one direction you are greeted by cascading hills of the woods that surround the lovely Valley Forge Park adding a green serenity in the summer and stunning blankets of white in the winter. In the other direction is the opposite view, 21st century madness as all you can observe are the crowds and cars rushing in and out of the King of Prussia mall, bags in hand, buying what the commercials on television tell them they can't live without.

Within our office, the sound of commerce and the daily grind dominated the soundscape with the hustle and bustle of smart, aggressive people going at their tasks a million miles an hour. My business partner, Jeffrey Erb and I had founded a company a few years prior called Supply Marketing that sold advertising on medical products with a primary emphasis on the great large white sheets in every doctor's office, the examination table paper. But that was not our only love. Jeff and I shared a mistress, one that could enter our thoughts without a seconds notice, and not leave until we satisfied her many demands. We both shared a love for Movies. We have since taken that passion to the next level after the sale of Supply Marketing with the creation of Framelight Productions, but that, along with a few other topics in this note, is a tale for another day.

Now the day in recall, I remember as any other day, nothing out of the ordinary. The birds were chirping, one of our sales ladies Terri, could be heard in the distance talking to this client or that, and our investor and land lord, Dr. Bennett was prowling the floor of the office looking for more deals to feed his expanding business. I was in my office, the cool one with the great art and photographs, right besides Jeff's, and as we were prone to do, he and I were sending film information to each other, sharing introductions to films that we thought the other had not had heard of but would enjoy. Recently, I had stumbled upon *Les Vampires* by Louis Feuillade and immediately thought of my close friend and business partner. What many people believe is that Jeff is the ultimate expert of vampire movies, products and history. Not true. His real expertise is in all things vodka but I'm sworn to secrecy on that topic, so we'll move on closing this sidebar discussion, but bear in mind that he is infrequently seen by day, always has beautiful woman hypnotically drawn to him and rocks the black clothes, so there may be a reason why vampires resonate so deeply with him. On the day I am recalling, I sent Jeff an email about the film *Les Vampires* which he promptly read, ordered a copy on Amazon and dove into researching it, when he suddenly came into my office with a link he wanted me to see. I recall the sunlight behind him, giving him a sort of glow as he said he found something I would like. I vaguely recall an angelic choir singing, but as we rarely saw angels in our King of Prussia office, I tend to dismiss this part of the memory. Then he said, he found a film by the same director about a character that he thought would be right up my alley.

Something called *Judex*.

I had never heard of *Judex*, so I started reading the history of him online. All day, I kept finding more and more until this avenger in black who had magically captivated my imagination. That night at home, I found myself still thinking about him, to the point where I started to see this film in my head. Then fate stepped in as the next day during my search, I learned that a west coast company called Flicker Alley had introduced it on DVD for the first time *that very week*, (a sign from the gods) so I ordered a copy. Then providence struck again as I found a copy of the 1963 remake by Georges Franju from Philly based Movies Unlimited and ordered one of those. But it took a week for them to arrive so in the interim, I begun to draft a story of the character based on internet "facts." In hindsight, the writers of these pages I doubt ever saw the films as little about the characters, plots and stories were correct. But they were fascinating. I knew that the characters sounded out of the ordinary and the elements to the story were unlike anything I had read. Sure, the death of his father as an inspiration for his revenge was kinda like Batman, and the slouch hat made him look like the Shadow, but he wasn't avenging all crime, just his father's death, and he didn't turn the bad guys over the cops, he kept them in his own prison. That was exciting because it was different. Then there were interesting characters like Favraux, Cocantin, Jacqueline, the Licorice Kid, Diana Monti and Robert

Morales (that I misread because I thought they were Favraux's henchmen, but for my purposes it worked out) that I found captivating.

So I sat down and banged out a rough first draft. It was okay and the foundation was there, but it wasn't what it could be. Then the mailman arrived and two days in a row he had packages for me. A DVD from Flicker Alley and a VHS from Movies Unlimited both with the story of a French avenger. I made a martini my way (3 parts Zyr vodka, 2 parts Bombay Sapphire gin, 1 part Lillet with a lemon garnish—James Bond for you purist likes his with gin then vodka, unless it is from a grain not potato but we'll discuss that over cocktails when you are buying), lit up a Macanudo 1968, popped the DVD in before settling in my comfortable chair. From the opening notes of the new score by Robert Israel, I was transported to France just before the First World War. Here, in these newly cleaned prints, I watched all 12 chapters of Feuillade's masterpiece, learning who the characters were and that Judex really was the father of many of our modern masked vigilantes. He had his own secret hideaway, tools, costume, an arch nemesis, side-kicks and a pledged purpose. But he was fresh and new while being old and inspirational. Then I watched Franju's take on the character and he went a little more surreal with him with the birds head masks and similarly attired assistants in slouch hats and capes. I knew what I had to do. I had no choice anymore. Mr. Feuillade had taken over my body and I was compelled to write an up-dated story of *Judex*. My take had to be different as I was moving him from France to Philadelphia and from the 1900s to 2000s. I had my work cut out and dove into this, writing *Judex* in my free time.

Judex is a tough property to adapt. I know a few major Hollywood producers who explored it, but the biggest problem is Batman. No matter how you slice it, it comes up looking and smelling like Batman. I tried to avoid that, but, looking back, I didn't. I have a fresh take on this iconic character, but the son of Thomas and Martha Wayne is in his DNA.

Give this script a fair read. It was my first complete work and was truly a labor of love. I had help on writing it from friends and family all sharing opinions, but along the way of writing this screenplay, I fell in love with the characters, the story and the potential. A year or so after writing my script, in *Tales of the Shadowmen* (Volume Three), I created a story called "The Two Hunters." This took place in the city of my dreams, Paris circa 1915 and featured Judex with Lord Greystoke. To my surprise, I received notes and emails from people all around the world who liked that story and wanted more. They liked how I was true to both Feuillade and Burroughs heroes and tried to show them as equals in an unequal world. Those notes made me smile. Not as much as giving my family and my parents a copy of TOTS 3 and watching them beam, but it was a close second.

Beware. If you have wronged anyone and think you have escaped justice, think again. You didn't for in the shadows coming for you is JUDEX!

Robert L. Robinson, Jr.

FADE IN

The screen is pitch black. In blazing white letters the screen reveals:

TEXT

"Judex ergo cum sedebit
Quidquid latet apparebit.
Nil inultum remanebit."

DISSOLVE TO:

SECOND BUMPER

TEXT

"When therefore the Judge takes His seat
Whatever is hidden will reveal itself.
Nothing will remain unavenged."
-- Requiem by Mozart

FADE OUT.

PHILADELPHIA SKYLINE - DUSK

TEXT

15 Years ago...

DISSOLVE TO:

Tomorrow night.

A storm prepares to rage in the distance. Thunder roars announcing its arrival, sirens wail, and the wind howls as lightning bolts rape the pre-evening sky. Somewhere in the distance a church bell begins to toll.

The camera opens with a close up on a rose. We hold here then pull back slightly to reveal that the rose is part of a bouquet. We then pull back slightly to see that the bouquet is laying in front of a grave. With a slight pull back we then see the grave is in the middle of a cemetery. We have various slow dollies through the cemetery finally showing in the distance the city behind it. Philadelphia. Moving forward, the camera explores streets of the inner city, making its way to the heart of the city. All the while, showing the people, the lifeblood of the city, illustrating the good and bad in man, as it makes it' way to a magnificent building. It then begins a slow pan up this structure of steel and glass.

INT. OFFICE BUILDING
The camera slowly travels down a long corridor of a dark and closed office. The people that normally would be at work are now at home or play as their day is done, leaving their desks and cubicles empty. The camera continues until it reaches the office it seeks.

WILLIAM TREMEUSE'S OFFICE – INTERIOR VIEW
The office is elegant, obviously the domain of a successful person. The trappings of success are about the room.

As the camera moves across the room from right to left, we see a man at his desk.

Standing before the desk is another man. A man, who would be imposing no matter how large and towering, stands tall, dominating the other. Both men are seen in the shadows as the room is dimly lit. They each are wearing expensive suits, very professionally attired.

One man, the larger, RICHARD FAVRAUX, is enjoying his victory, the pleasure shown through his confident, almost arrogant posturing. The other man, WILLIAM TREMEUSE, is a man who is not used to defeat. He has suffered his first, a horrible, humiliating defeat and is broken. He is hunched over his desk, not looking directly at the man who broke him, not sure if it is over, praying inside himself that it is not.

Behind the seated large man are two women. They are stunning and attractive. We never learn their names. The large man is standing tall before the desk, looming over the man in the chair.

FAVRAUX

It's over.

The man behind the desk says nothing and looks up with dead eyes at the large man. A symbol of all that he worked for is represented by the office and the company that his family founded. It is lost now. Lost to the man before him.

FAVRAUX (cont'd)
I will replace your board with mine and my man
will assume your position.

WILLIAM TREMEUSE
What will you do with my company?

While talking to the man in the chair, the larger man removes a cigar from his pocket and goes through the mo-
tions of opening the wrap about it, slowly and carefully
with an expensive clipper, cutting off the end, then twirl-
ing the cigar under his nose, to breathe in the aroma of
the leaf.

FAVRAUX
Break it up, sell off the pieces.

WILLIAM TREMEUSE
But I have employees, Favraux. People that have
been with my family for years. Doesn't that
mean anything to you?

FAVRAUX
They are casualties, Tremeuse. It is that simple.
There are always casualties.

One of the two women behind the large man, steps forward with a lighter and lights the cigar, the flame from
the expensive lighter illuminating his face. An evil smile
crosses his mouth, as he slowly draws in on the imported
cigar.

FAVRAUX(cont'd)
You, my friend, are now a casualty.

He has no compassion, no feelings of sympathy for the people that will lose their jobs. He only feels a perverse pleasure at his victory.

FAVRAUX(cont'd)
Enjoy tonight. It is your last in this office.

The large man exhales a cloud of smoke and turns and walks to the door without looking back. The two women follow him silently. What is behind him physically is behind him in life. He gives it no more thought. Tremeuse's company is now his and his mind is off to his next conquest.

Tremeuse sits behind the desk simply watching the large man and his entourage, as he opens the door, steps through it and closes it behind them. The man behind the desk rises shakily, then goes over to a radio and turns it on.

Classical music fills the room, the sounds from Mozarts's *Requiem*, *Rex tremendae*, playing in the background as the thunder and church bells in the distance accompany it. The music has rolling themes and cascading voices that Tremeuse reacts to. He closes his eyes, his hands gently swaying in the air as if conducting an invisible orchestra.

Tremeuse then moves across the room to the bar he keeps in his office and takes out a short glass, then reaches into an ice tub. He takes out a handful of ice, dropping the ice in a short glass, one cube at a time, each clinking and tinkling when they hit.

To complete the action, Tremeuse then reaches for a crystal decanter filled with scotch and pours deliberately and methodically into his glass. He slowly rolls the scotch around the glass in his hand, the ice cracking from the warmth of the liquid, as he walks about his office.

He turns to return to his desk, this the first time we see his face clearly. Sweat covers his body as he sits behind the desk. He straightens up the items on his desk, removes a sheet of personal stationary, uses his fountain pen to methodically write a short note. He folds the note, puts it in an envelope that he places in his inside breast pocket of his jacket, then puts the pen back in place.

He looks about the room taking in the sights of his family and his accomplishments. He reaches into a brief case and places a revolver on the desk. Looking at the gun, he sips his drinks twice, then in one last gulp, finishes the drink. He slowly runs his hand along the gun, his fingers gently sweeping across the cold metal. His eyes close in a silent meditation as he makes a final decision.

                    WILLIAM TREMEUSE
          Forgive me...

We have begun the FADE TO BLACK as the explosion roars, ending with the screen fully black.

                                        IRIS OUT.

ROLL CREDITS.

The credits flicker as if a silent movie. Each individual credit listed on a silent movie title card.

FADE OUT.

PRISON EXT VIEW DAYTIME
Establishing shot of the facility.

PRISON INT VIEW DAYTIME
View inside of the prison, cold, dirty and evil. In a cell, a man stands upright, over another man. This is the warden, JOHN PINKERTON. On the cold floor, a man possessed does push ups. Push up after push up, his body a machine. While not a young man any more, he has the body of a sculpted athlete. This is CAL HULLEN who appears to be a man half his age of fifty.

PINKERTON
Tomorrow is your last day in here, Hullen.

HULLEN
Ten years.

PINKERTON
Ten years. That's a long time.

Hullen says nothing but continues the up and down motion of the push ups. His muscular arms glistening from the sweat that covers them, pumping like pistons.

PINKERTON (cont'd)
Some men break the first day.

HULLEN
(Eyes just glare at him)

PINKERTON
You didn't. You survived.

HULLEN
(Eyes just glare at him)

Hullen stops doing the push ups in the down position, his arms locked. He looks up into the eyes of the warden. The strain on his arms intense.

PINKERTON
Remember, Hullen, most men who walk out these doors, usually return through them.

HULLEN
(Eyes just glare at him)

PINKERTON
Good luck then.

Hullen returns to the pushups. The warden exits. Hullen stops, picks up a towel dries himself off. Adjacent to Hullen, hanging on the wall are newspaper and magazine articles that cover the bricks. All about Favraux. He starts ripping them down, slowly, methodically, in control.

EXTERIOR PHILADELPHIA ACADEMY OF MUSIC – DUSK
Yellow lights illuminate the outside of the grand building. The light fights off the coming darkness for the

shadowed patrons entering the hall. Up the stately stair-well the length of the building, high society elegantly dressed for a performance, enter the hall.

INT. PHILADELPHIA ACADEMY OF MUSIC
The audience waits in anticipation, reading and rattling programs.

INT. PHILADELPHIA ACADEMY OF MUSIC – MAIN STAGE
The lights dim and the curtain goes up and the opera starts.

INT. PHILADELPHIA ACADEMY OF MUSIC – PRIVATE BOX
Inside a dark spectator box, sits a man and a woman attired in formal wear. Both are attractive and elegantly attired. The couple is JACK TREMEUSE and his date, RANDI SIRKIN. They sit enjoying the music while sipping champagne. Alone in the box, the lights from the stage dance off their faces as the music fills the air. The first act of the opera ends.

                    RANDI
          That was beautiful.

                    JACK
          It's one of my favorites. My parents introduced
          it to my brother and I when we were young.

                    RANDI
          It's too sad for children.

JACK
Sometimes, children can't avoid the sadness.

RANDI
But this story is about unfulfilled love.

JACK
So is life.

RANDI
Spoken from experience?

A knock on the door to the box stops the conversation. Jack rises to open it. The door opens and a MESSENGER with a note steps in.

MESSENGER
Mr. Jack Tremeuse?

JACK
Yes...

The messenger hands a sealed envelope to Tremeuse, who reaches into his pocket, takes out a money clip and peels off a twenty dollar bill that he hands to the man.

MESSENGER
Thank you, sir.

Tremeuse opens the envelope, reads the note then folds it, placing it in his breast pocket. He drains his glass and bends down to kiss Randi. She looks up with a disappointed look in her eyes.

RANDI

You've got to be kidding Jack? It's only the first act.

JACK

If this was any other client, I wouldn't move an inch.

RANDI

Don't you leave.

JACK

You're going to have to take my word.

RANDI

Jack (drawn out way of saying it)

JACK

I'm sorry, but I have no choice.

Jack walks out. Randi sits back, seething, slamming her purse against his seat in anger.

EXT. PHILADELPHIA ACADEMY OF MUSIC PARKING GARAGE

A valet brings an expensive sports car to the exit of the parking garage. Jack tips the valet, enters the car and speeds away.

SMALL TOWN AMERICA – ROCK HALL, MARYLAND – DUSK

A town that has escaped time. It looks now as it did ten years ago, twenty years ago, or even forty years ago. Clean streets with friendly people walking down them.

Jack Tremeuse's black Ferrari pulls into town. Jack gets out of the car and walks down the road, looking around as he walks. He notices a car repair garage, now out of business. Standing, looking at the abandoned shop, he pauses. He sees his reflection in the window of the shop, his mind comes back to where he is, then he walks in.

<u>INT. ICE CREAM SHOP – DUSK</u>
Jack walks into an ice cream shop smiling a hello to the various people sitting and working. He walks to a booth along the left side wall, across from the greeting cards. WAITRESS walks over.

WAITRESS

Hi there.

JACK

Hello.

WAITRESS

Can I get you a menu?

JACK

No thanks, I know just what I want. I'd like one your famous strawberry milk shakes, extra thick.

WAITRESS

One of our famous strawberry milk shakes, extra thick, coming right up.

The waitress turns and walks away. Jack Tremeuse sits and stares out the window. He is lost in thought.

On a country road just outside of town, William Tremeuse stands over his overheated car engine. His wife, ANN TREMEUSE and their two sons, JACK and ROGER, sit in the car. William tosses his jacket down on the ground in disgust.

ANN
Maybe we need a new battery?

William shakes his head in frustration, unscrews the radiator cap and burns his arm.

WILLIAM
Owwww!

A man, CAL HULLEN, and his son, RUDY, walk up to the car. Cal and Rudy dressed in overalls, give the appearance of poverty.

HULLEN
You either need some water for that radiator or some salve for that burn.

WILLIAM
Most likely, both.

HULLEN
I can probably fix the car better than I can your arm.

WILLIAM
I'd be grateful for anything that you can do.

HULLEN

What brings you down here?

WILLIAM

We were sailing out of Great Oaks up the road,
and I was bringing the kids into Rock Hall for
shakes. Well, until this happened...
          (extending hand)
Thank you, Mr...?

HULLEN

Name's Hullen, Cal Hullen. This is my boy,
Rudy.

WILLIAM

Mine's Bill. Bill Tremeuse.

HULLEN

          (looking at car while talking)
Might take a day or so.

WILLIAM

A day? I have a board meeting back in Philadelphia tomorrow.

HULLEN

Hmmmmm. That might be a problem. Could try
to get it patched enough to get you folks on your
way tonight, or...

WILLIAM

How about you take a shot at it?

HULLEN

Fine. Rudy, take the Missus and the boys back to the house and have mom fix them a meal. We'll take care of you till we can get you back on the road.

ANN

You're very kind.

WILLIAM

I appreciate the offer. How much is it going to be...?

HULLEN

Don't you worry none about money. Rudy, take these folks back on home and let me and Mr. Bill get this car off the road.

INT. HULLEN HOUSE – LATER

William and Ann Tremeuse and Lisa Hullen finish up a meal as the three boys play outside on a tire swing.

ANN

That was just wonderful.

WILLIAM

I can't imagine anywhere in the world, where we could have been so lucky.

LISA

That's the way Cal is. He doesn't have his job no more, but it don't matter. He'd still give you his last nickel, if he thought you needed it.

WILLIAM
How long has he been out of work?

LISA
Almost six months. There's only one factory around these parts, Favraux Machines, and he got himself fired when one of the bosses was takin' more than he should have from his check. Cal tried to speak to him about it, but it was a very short talk I hear.

WILLIAM
I know Richard Favraux. I didn't know he was down in these parts.

LISA
He owns most everything down here.

ANN
That's horrible about Cal. And he can't find another job?

LISA
Times are tight down here. We all work for the farmer to stay afloat, but I know Cal. He'd like to open a little garage or something, strike out on his own, y'know what I mean.

EXT. HULLEN HOUSE – CONTINUOUS
Rudy, Roger, and Jack skim stones on a creek.

YOUNG ROGER
You got a baseball field around here?

RUDY

'Course we do. But I don't play.

YOUNG JACK

You don't play baseball?

RUDY

My daddy said he ain't got the money to buy me a glove.

YOUNG ROGER

You do go to school?

RUDY

Sometimes. When I ain't working in the fields.

YOUNG ROGER

You're a farmer?

RUDY

We work for a farmer. But one day I'm shakin' the dirt off me like your daddy and that big shot that owns the factory. I'll be rich too.

YOUNG JACK

What big shot?

RUDY

Mr. Favraux. He owns the factory and most everything down here. He must be the richest man in the world.

The boys sit in the car while Ann and Lisa exchange good byes. William and Cal stand in front of the repaired car.

WILLIAM
I can't thank you and your family enough.

HULLEN
It'll get you home okay. Have your mechanic really give it a go over though.

William hands him a check.

WILLIAM
You should be fixing cars full time.

Cal takes check and looks at it and then to Lisa.

HULLEN
No, sir, I couldn't...

WILLIAM
Look, get yourself that garage. Get a start.

HULLEN
I hardly know you, I can't take your charity.

WILLIAM
You didn't know me, but you helped me without a second thought. Look, this isn't charity. It's an investment. A good investment in a good man.

HULLEN

I don't know what to say.

WILLIAM

Just say yes.

In the back of the car, the boys are talking to each other during the above dialog.

YOUNG ROGER

Hey Rudy!

Rudy walks over to the car.

Jack throws something out of the window at him. Rudy catches it and looks at it. It is a baseball glove. Then Roger throws something at him. Rudy catches it in the glove. It is a ball.

YOUNG JACK

Next time we come down, we'll play catch!

RUDY

You betcha!

INT. TREMEUSE CAR – CONTINUOUS

William starts the car and drives away from the house. Ann and William's eyes meet and she smiles as she puts her hand on his leg.

YOUNG ROGER

Daddy, is Rudy's family going to be okay?

WILLIAM
> Yes they are. I think that they are going to be fine.

INT. RESTAURANT PRESENT DAY – CONTINUOUS
Jack comes out of thought, finishes his milkshake. He stands up, leaves a tip for the waitress and exits.

INT. COURT ROOM – MID MORNING
JUDGE WEXLER presides over a trial. A jury of twelve sits to the side while at tables before the bench, the defense team sits led by attorney, ALICE SHAPIRO. Prosecuting attorney, ROGER TREMEUSE, sits across the aisle. On trial is ARCHIE HINTON. Sitting in the crowd are DAVID and BETSY GAINES. DETECTIVES KINAHAN and COCANTIN are there but not together.

SHAPIRO
> Ladies and gentlemen of the jury, in the last several weeks you have seen the prosecution make one mistake after another. We have discovered that the evidence presented by Detective Kinahan was mishandled at the very least and possibly tainted. We have shown that key witnesses were pressured by police to give statements...

While Shapiro addresses the jury, District Attorney Roger Tremeuse wanders off in a daydream.

FLASHBACK INT. FUNERAL PARLOR – DAY
Inside a funeral parlor, William Tremeuse's casket sits. A line of people approach the casket to pay their re-

spects, while Ann Tremeuse and her sons stand a silent vigil beside his body. Finally, Ann and her sons are alone with William's body. Jack and Roger step forward. Both kneel down for a last good bye. Jack puts in a soccer ball that he had on the ground near them. Roger stands silently with a tear in his eye. His mother tries to pull him away but Roger won't leave.

> ANN
> Roger, we have to say good bye now, honey.

> YOUNG ROGER
> I'm going to stay with Dad.

> ANN
> Come on, sweetie, Daddy has to sleep now. We can't stay.

INT. COURTROOM – CONTINUOUS
Roger wakes up from his daydream and continues listening to Shapiro.

> SHAPIRO
> And in conclusion ladies and gentlemen of the jury, I ask you to remember the following: The evidence the police presented was tainted and Judge Wexler ruled it was not admissible. There is nothing that ties my client to the murder of John Gaines. The only verdict you can come back with is finding my client Not Guilty. Thank you.

Shapiro walks around to her table and sits down. Hinton whispers something in her ear. She looks away with a disgusted look on her face.

Roger Tremeuse stands and walks in front of the bench then looks at the Jury.

ROGER

Archie Hinton, no matter how you look at it is a bad person. He has inflicted pain on others all his life. As an adult this has not changed. What has changed unfortunately is the magnitude of his crimes.

> (He points out to the couple in the stands watching the trial)

Those are the parents of John Gaines. John Gaines will never graduate from college while his parents look in pride. John Gaines will never get married nor will his mother cry at his wedding. Why? Because she cried at his funeral. She cried at his grave site. She cries every day. She cries because that man...

> (he points at Hinton)

Archie Hinton, killed her son. He killed him because he walked into the wrong place at the wrong time and saw Hinton doing harm to someone else. You have seen the defense tell you that the police had bad evidence. It was good when they collected it, but somehow, someway, something happened to taint it.

SHAPIRO

Your honor...

                    JUDGE WEXLER
        Tread carefully counselor.

Roger looks at the Judge, not pleased with him. He is in
front of the jury box.

                       ROGER
        You twelve members of the Jury must see be-
        yond what "truth" they want you to see. You
        must come to the real truth yourself. I quote Jus-
        tice Earl Warren who said: "It is the spirit and
        not the form of the law that keeps justice alive."
        You twelve members of the Jury, are the body of
        the law, and as such have to keep Justice alive.
        See through the charade presented to you and
        find this evil man guilty. Thank you.

Roger walks to his table and sits down.

EXT. CHURCH BUILDING – DUSK
Silhouette shot of church framed in the early evening
light.

INT. CHURCH BUILDING
The church has few patrons in it. The camera moves
slowly past random parishioners engaged in prayer until
resting before a confessional. Slowly the camera moves
closer.

INT. CONFESSIONAL
The room is darkened. We see The PRIEST in the foreground, but behind the screen, hidden in the shadows is a
man. We cannot see him clearly. He is JUDEX, but not
in costume. He wears a dark hat, the large brim keeping

his face hidden, while black sunglasses cover his eyes. The audience still is not to know who he is.

JUDEX

Bless me Father, for I will sin.

PRIEST

Will sin?

JUDEX

It has been... well... it's been a while since my last confession.

PRIEST

That is a long time between confessions my son.

JUDEX

It is.

PRIEST

Begin my son...

JUDEX

I'm not here to ask for forgiveness, Father.

PRIEST

I'm confused then. Don't you want me to hear your confession?

JUDEX

I'm not here to confess.

PRIEST

No?

JUDEX

No. I'm here to ask a question.

PRIEST

You didn't have to come into a confessional to ask it.

JUDEX

It seemed appropriate.

PRIEST

Well then, what can I help you with?

JUDEX

I want revenge, Father.

PRIEST

I offer forgiveness.

JUDEX

I know. But tell me, is there room in Hell for an evil man that has ruined many lives?

PRIEST

I can only speak of Heaven my son. There is always room there for a child of God. Are you asking me for permission to harm this man? I am a man of God and would not grant it.

JUDEX

I didn't come to ask for permission.

PRIEST

Then why did you come?

JUDEX

I came, I guess, more or less to say goodbye.

PRIEST

Goodbye? Good bye to who?

JUDEX

God.

PRIEST

God? No my son, God never says goodbye.
Think over what you want to do. Revenge is
wrong. Jesus teaches us in the gospels to love
our enemies.

JUDEX

Then Jesus can love them, but I can't.

PRIEST

Who are you to take this role unto yourself? Only God's Archangels may wield the fiery sword.

JUDEX

I am Judex.

PRIEST

I'll pray for you Judex. I'll pray that you find
peace in your soul and that this plan for revenge
will be replaced by love. I'll pray for this to The
Virgin Mary, Holy Mother of God, and the an-

gels and saints and to the Father, the Son and the Holy Spirit.

JUDEX

Amen.

FAVRAUX'S MANSION EXT SHOT NIGHT
Expensive cars fill the drive and the surrounding grounds. The sounds of a party fill the air.

FAVRAUX'S MANSION INT LIVING ROOM
The guests are all in beautiful clothes. In the crowd we see Randi Sirkin and others. The lively sounds of a band play in the background. The camera follows a WAITER with a tray of drinks through the crowd. As he passes a doorway, the camera leaves the waiter and focuses on the door.

FAVRAUX'S MANSION INT HOUSE THE WINE CELLAR
Down a flight of steps to a large wine cellar filled with wines and bottles of all age and types. A humidor is in the distance and a tasting table is near the entrance. Seated and standing about the table are six people and at the head of the table is Favraux.

These people are DAVID HOLLAND, who runs the street gangs in Philadelphia; ALAN GIORDANIO, who represents the Italian mafia in Philadelphia; JIMMY MARLEY, who runs the Jamaican gangs in Philadelphia; JOHN LAMB, who runs a large investment firm that is part of the stock exchange in Philadelphia; and ZHOU ZHI-RO who represents her father, who has taken over the Asian gangs in Philadelphia.

At the other end of the table, a woman sits that does not talk. Her name is JENNY COCANTIN. She is a corrupt police official that works for Favraux.

The guests dress goes from the extreme of suits of hip hop culture to the board room chic.

Behind him stand both DIANA MONTI and ROBERTA MORALES. Both are stunning and beautiful in their gowns. Where he goes, they go.

                    FAVRAUX
          I have guests upstairs to return to.

                    HOLLAND
          We have a big problem Mr. Favraux.

                    FAVRAUX
          What is it?

Lamb reaches into his jacket and takes out a gavel. He hands it to Favraux.

                    LAMB
          We've each had a visitor. I can't afford visitors like this one, Richard. Our relationship has to stay behind closed doors, yet he came to us with a message for you.

                    FAVRAUX
                    (puzzled)
          A message. What did he say?

INT. RECORDING STUDIO – PREVIOUS NIGHT

Holland sits at a mixer while a hip hop artist records from a sound booth behind glass. Holland intermittently takes a hit from a hand rolled cigarette while he moves to the beat of the music in his headset. In the sound booth we see the rapper doing his thing into the microphone as the music blares in the background. Sitting in mixing room are TWO TECHNICIANS, and Holland, the producer. The music hits a note and ends. Holland leans over to the microphone.

HOLLAND
That's it brother. You hit that jam.

RAPPER
(He simply nods his head)

Everyone gets up, and walks to a room with drinks and food.

From out of nowhere, a black flash races forward with a long gavel. He is on the Rapper and the two technicians quickly, taking them down. He turns his attention to Holland. The figure in black slowly moves forward. Holland does not look happy as he steps backwards. All the while, we never clearly see the man in black.

Then the shape in the black is upon him. Three bodies lie on the floor unconscious. Lying alive on the floor is David Holland, while kneeling down above him, holding him up with his lapels is a man in black. Long white hair, hangs down covering his masked face, as he leans in close to Holland, so that there is no mistaking his intentions. He pulls Holland close to his face as he speaks to him.

> JUDEX
> Tell Favraux that Justice is coming for him.

> HOLLAND
> Who are you?

> JUDEX
> I am Judex.

The man in black drops a gavel onto Holland.

INT. WINE CELLAR

We are back to the wine cellar at Favraux's. Holland has just finished telling his story, and hands Favraux the gavel he was given. The men all nod in agreement as similar events have happened to them. Zhou takes out her gavel.

> ZHOU
> This masked man, he has disturbed our business. We need to kill him.

EXT. WAREHOUSE ON WATERFRONT – PREVIOUS NIGHT

Zhou and two associates, clandestinely, break into a warehouse and load stolen freight from a forklift onto a waiting truck. They speak in Chinese.

From Zhou's frightened expression signals something dangerous has descended. Zhou snaps her fingers and her two associates immediately descend upon the visitor.

The visitor in rapid succession easily handles the two associates with two quick kicks and a flurry of punches. Judex pulls her in tight.

                    JUDEX
        Tell Favraux that Justice is coming.

The man in black drops a gavel onto Zhou.

INT. WINE CELLAR
All are still sitting around the table.

                    FAVRAUX
        That's all he said, "Justice is coming?"

INT. LUXURY PENTHOUSE – PREVIOUS NIGHT
Giordano engaged in sex under the covers of a bed. As he climaxes and rolls over, the detached prostitute waits a beat, gets out of the bed, throws on a robe, kisses him and heads for the bathroom.

                    PROSTITUTE
        You were so good, I should pay you.

                    GIORDANIO
        I'll bet you say that to all your clients.

                    PROSTITUTE
        I would if they were as good as you, sugar.

She exits. Giordano lights a cigarette, sits back with a satisfied expression, inhales and exhales. His eyes light up, seeing someone enter the room. He quickly jumps out of bed and scrambles to put on a robe. We see the shape in black attack Giordano.

JUDEX
Tell Favraux that Justice is coming for him.

The man in black drops a gavel onto Giordanio.

FAVRAUX'S MANSION. INT. WINE CELLAR.
We are back to the wine cellar at Favraux's. Giordanio hands Favraux his gavel. Others about the room all take out theirs.

GIORDANIO
He had on some kind of crazy mask. Real long face, everything covered up. I can't tell you if he was white or black.

FAVRAUX
Somewhere along the way we knew we would make enemies. Fine. We have an enemy in black. But, he is a man. And men bleed and can die. Now, is there anything else or may I return to my guests?

ZHOU
We are completed. If you say you have this un-der control, that is all I need to hear.

MARLEY
Under control? You balls afraid and ain't doing nothing.

FAVRAUX

We just learned of this Judex. Have patience Mr.
Marley.

MARLEY

You have to find this man and kill him! If you
can't do that, then why am me and my people
muleing for you?

FAVRAUX

Mr. Marley, may I see your gun for a minute?
        (beat)
I don't often have a need to hold one.

Marley takes out the gun and hands it to Favraux.
Favraux examines it closely, showing that he does know
how to handle a gun, then turns and places the barrel
between Holland's eyes.

MARLEY

Hey man, that gun is loaded. Don't be playing.

FAVRAUX

        (lowering the gun)
You are right of course Mr. Marley. I wouldn't
want to play with a loaded gun.

Favraux holds out the gun for Marley to take, which he
does.

MARLEY

        (laughing)
I knew you couldn't kill no one mon.

Favraux turns his back to begin for the door, Marley gains strength when Favraux has his back to him.

                    MARLEY (cont'd)
          You think the name Favraux means anything
          where I come from?

Favraux looks at the ladies, who immediately attack Marley with a lightning attack of brutality and savagery not expected from two beautiful women.

Favraux stands over the now dead Marley looking down.

                    FAVRAUX
          It will now.

Favraux looks about the room. Then something goes off in his head.

                    FAVRAUX (cont'd)
          We're missing a few members of our organiza-
          tion, aren't we?

                    GIORDANIO
          They're missing.

                    FAVRAUX
          Missing?

                    GIORDANIO
          Friggin' vanished off the face of the Earth.

FAVRAUX

There is more to this. Talk to the streets, see what is being said. I want to know what happened to our associates. And Mr. Holland...

HOLLAND

Yes?

FAVRAUX

You will take over Marley's businesses for us.

The people around the table nod, then all get up to leave. One at a time, they leave the room, stepping over and around Marley.

Cocantin stays behind for a moment, as she always does. Favraux places a hand gently but firmly on her arm as he walks past her.

FAVRAUX (cont'd)

Sometimes it takes a policeman to do what a gangster can't. Learn what you can about this Judex.

Cocantin nods her head then leaves. Favraux extends his arms and both ladies take either side of him, their arms locked into his.

FAVRAUX (cont'd)

My Valkyries.

INT. STAIRWAY FROM WINE CELLAR – MOMENTS LATER

Favraux, Monti and Morales enter the party from stairwell. The crowded party burst with excitement as revelers in evening attire merrily drink, eat, and dance. Favraux, with his mistresses at his side, circulates mixing with all of Philadelphia's high society. John Lamb comes from behind and taps Favraux on the shoulder.

> FAVRAUX
>
> Yes?

> LAMB
>
> We need to talk.

> FAVRAUX
>
> The matter has been settled.

> LAMB
>
> But, we can't afford not to deal with this. People are vanishing, you are being threatened... I am being visited by some freak in the night, giving me gavels.

> FAVRAUX
>
> John, I have the finest families in Philadelphia in my home to raise money for charity. We have a problem, and like other problems it will be dealt with.

Favraux and the women walk away.

FAVRAUX'S MANSION EXT OUTSIDE THE LIV-
ING ROOM
The party. Group shot just to establish from the outside
looking in at the crowd and merriment about. People
everywhere are having a great time. The food, drink and
music are wonderful and the cream of Philadelphia society is there. To the people in attendance, Favraux is a
businessman that has made his money, buying and sell-
ing companies. He really deals in souls. Buying and de-
stroying them.

Jack Tremeuse walks through the party and bumps into
his old date, Randi Sirkin. Randi, with a happy buzz,
grabs two champagnes from a passing waiter. Jack takes
one from her.

                    JACK
    I'm sorry about the other night, Randi.

                    RANDI
    I'm having a good time tonight Jack. Lots of
    other men here that will actually stay through a
    date with me.

                    JACK
    I had no choice. I'm sorry.

                    RANDI
    I'm sure you are, but if I plan to hang around
    with you all night, you'll probably leave early
    and I'll have to hitchhike home.

Randi spies a friend from somewhere else and walks
away from Jack. He scans the room. His eyes fall on a

beautiful woman standing alone across the room. He stares and their eyes meet. He lifts his champagne glass to her. Jack takes the opportunity and crosses the room to the stand alone woman.

She is stunning and, surprisingly, alone. The lady is JACQUELINE AUBREY.

> JACK
> That is a lovely gown.

> JACQUELINE
> Thank you. You can't go wrong with Nicole Miller.

> JACK
> Tell that to Holstein.

> JACQUELINE
> Are you in the fashion business, Mister...?

> JACK
> Tremeuse...Jack Tremeuse.

> JACQUELINE
> Tremeuse... Your name... is it French?

> JACK
> *Oui. Mes ancêtres sont originaires du Nord de la France. Ils ont émigré avant qu'on ait commence à décapiter les Nobles et sont devenus de vrais Américains, je suis assez fier de le dire.*
> (in English Subtitles)

Yes. My family originally was from Northern France, but came to the colonies before nobles were beheaded to begin their lives as Americans, I am proud to say.

JACQUELINE

J'aime l'Europe. J'y ai vécu depuis l'âge de trois ans, après le décès de ma mère. Mon père m'a mis dans un internat en Suisse. J'ai passé toutes mes vacances d'été avec lui à Paris, jusqu'à mon départ pour l'université.

(In English Subtitles)

I love Europe. I lived there since I was three, when my mother passed away. My father sent me to a boarding school in Switzerland. My summers, I spent in Paris with him, until I went to college.

JACK

J'ai fait mes études en Suisse également. Que le monde est petit! Aimez-vous la France?

(In English Subtitles)

I spent my college years in Switzerland also. What a small world it is. Did you enjoy France?

JACQUELINE

Oui. J'y retourne presque chaque année. Après l'université, j'ai travaillé à l'ambassade américaine à Paris. Travaillez-vous dans l'international?

(In English Subtitles)

I did. I have returned almost every year. After college I worked in the American Embassy in

Paris. Are you in international work of some sort?

JACK
Non, je travaille avec des sociétés en difficultés. Je les sauve des pirates de la finance.
(In English Subtitles)
No, I work with companies under fire. I rescue them from corporate raiders.

At this moment Favraux enters the scene. He obviously has a magnificent command of French.

FAVRAUX
Certaines personnes pensent que vous vous mêlez de ce qui ne vous regarde pas, Monsieur Tremeuse.
(In English Subtitles)
There are those that think you interfere, Mr. Tremeuse.

JACK
(Smiling and back to English)
Someone has to keep you honest, Mr. Favraux.

FAVRAUX
Just like your father, Mr. Tremeuse. An idealist.

Favraux has struck a raw nerve, but Jack will not let him see it. He returns his focus to the woman that he is speaking with, trying to ignore Favraux.

JACK

So, you now know my name and what I do, but I
still know nothing about you.

FAVRAUX

Her name, Mr. Tremeuse, is Mrs. Jacqueline
Aubrey.

JACK

It is both my pleasure and bad timing to make
your acquaintance Mrs. Aubrey. Please forgive
my forwardness, as I had no idea you were married.
          (beat)
Your husband is indeed, a lucky man.

JACQUELINE

Thank you. But my husband passed away four
years ago. He was a good man, I was the lucky
one.

JACK

You have my deepest sympathies. I had no idea
of your loss. Please forgive my forwardness.

JACQUELINE

There's nothing to forgive. Please relax.

Monti leans over to whisper in Favraux's ear.

FAVRAUX

I will leave you two alone and return to my other
guests. (beat)

FAVRAUX (cont'd)
Tremeuse, I can trust you, can't I...with my most
prized possession?

Favraux once again has verbally floored Tremeuse. This
was an unexpected development. The two Valkyries take
Favraux's arms.

JACQUELINE
My lecherous father.

FAVRAUX
(laughing)
My lechery has served me well.

JACQUELINE
Most men would be satisfied with one voluptu-
ous woman.

FAVRAUX
I couldn't help it, They came as a pair. Now to
find your fiancé. I need to have a word with him.

JACQUELINE
I hope you have better luck finding him than I
had tonight.

FAVRAUX
Jacqueline... Tremeuse... enjoy the party.

Favraux kisses his daughter's cheek then turns without
looking at Tremeuse and walks away, arm in arm with
both Monti and Morales who smile a sexy, secret smile
at him.

JACQUELINE

I'm sorry Mr. Tremeuse, but my father can be a bit overbearing at times.

JACK

Jack, please...

JACQUELINE

Alright...Jack.

JACK

A father's love for his child is priceless.

JACQUELINE

It seems that you and my father have met.

JACK

We've had some...dealings together. I was going to invite you to dinner, but I did not know you were engaged.

JACQUELINE

You assumed that I am alone here tonight.

JACK

I'm full of mistakes tonight.

JACQUELINE

Are you always this forward?

JACK

Usually.

JACQUELINE
I like that. It's refreshing after all the games that go on here.

JACK
Sometimes it seems that all that goes on are games. Never just honest emotion.

JACQUELINE
A man that believes in emotion. That's different.

JACK
I'm different, that's for sure. Why not join me for lunch? See for yourself.

JACQUELINE
Maybe. Do you have a card?

Jack hands her a card. She accepts it and reads from it before placing it in her handbag.

JACK
I'll look forward to that.

EXT FAVRAUX MANSION STILL IN THE PARTY, GARDEN SHOT
In the garden talking to people are Favraux and his two mistresses at his side. Beautiful people in beautiful clothes surround him. Standing together are Favraux and Lamb chatting.

FAVRAUX
Our illustrious Mayor has just arrived.

LAMB

I think he's getting too big, too obvious. That corrupt fool could hurt us.

FAVRAUX

Count your blessings John. It is his corruptibility that benefits us.

MAYOR THOMAS JOHNSON, approaches Favraux and Lamb.

MAYOR JOHNSON

Richard, John, wonderful ball, wonderful! The highlight of my social calendar.

FAVRAUX

Thank you Mister Mayor. It is an honor that you attend each year.

MAYOR JOHNSON

And miss an opportunity to meet my biggest contributors. Men like you and Lamb here? Never.

LAMB

How are we doing on the wage tax issue, Mister Mayor? I have employees that are hoping to have it repealed.

MAYOR JOHNSON

John, you know how much revenue that tax brings in. You keep them happy, I keep you happy. That's the way it is. Always and forever.

A PRETTY BLOND in an extremely sexy gown walks by and the Mayor's head turns suddenly, following each sway and shake of her very shapely and sensuous behind.

>MAYOR JOHNSON (cont'd)
>Well gentlemen, it was a pleasure.

The Mayor turns to walk away, as Lamb and Favraux stand to chat.

>LAMB
>If he wasn't making us so much money, I would be done with that fool.

>FAVRAUX
>John, he's a politician. He can steal more money for us legally than we ever could. And most men who believe the power they were granted was earned, think with their little heads. That's why we can control the big head so easily.

Lamb walks away. Favraux turns to go back to the other guests when his phone rings. He reaches into his pocket and looks at the number. It is unknown and there are never any unknown numbers that call him.

>JUDEX (V.O.)
>You don't look as if you are enjoying your party.

>FAVRAUX
>But I am. I always enjoy spending time with my guests.

JUDEX (V.O.)
Which guests here will be your next victims Mr.
Favraux?

FAVRAUX
Ah, you must be Mr. Judex.

JUDEX (V.O.)
I am.

FAVRAUX
I received your messages.

JUDEX (V.O.)
I thought you might.

FAVRAUX
The gavels were a little extreme, but so is a
mask. What do you want?

JUDEX (V.O.)
Three billion, seven hundred and fifty million
dollars from your fortune donated to charity by
eight tomorrow night.

FAVRAUX
That's an unusual amount.

JUDEX (V.O.)
It is the amount you gained through blood and a
gun. Do you see the piano?

FAVRAUX
Yes.

JUDEX (V.O.)
Walk over to it. In the seat is a ledger. It details
every penny you stole and the interest owed.

Favraux while the conversation is going on, walks to the
piano, opens the seat and thumbs through the book. He
hands it to Monti.

FAVRAUX
And if I refuse?

JUDEX (V.O.)
By eight tomorrow.

FAVRAUX
I don't need one day, Mr. Judex.

JUDEX (V.O.)
Neither do I, Favraux.

Judex ends the call on his end. Favraux expected no less,
ponders for a moment, then turns to his ladies.

MONTI
Everything alright?

FAVRAUX
That was Judex on the phone.

MORALES
Judex? He's real?

FAVRAUX
Real enough to threaten me.

MONTI
Forget about him, we're watching your back.

MORALES
And your front.

They take him by the arm and go back into the party.

INT. FAVRAUX MANSION
Jack and Jacqueline are still chatting. Into their midst, Lamb comes over, places his arm around Aubrey, kisses her cheek, and then extends his other hand to Jack, who takes it.

LAMB
Jack.

JACK
John.

JACQUELINE
So you two know each other?

LAMB
Philadelphia is too small a town not to.

JACK
This lady might be more than you deserve, John.

LAMB

Why do you think that, Jack?

JACK

She walks in beauty, like the night
Of cloudless climes and starry skies;
And all that's best of dark and bright
Meet in her aspect and her eyes:
Thus mellow'd to that tender light
Which heaven to gaudy day denies.
One shade more, one ray less,
Had half impair'd the nameless grace
Which waves in every raven tress,
Or softly lightens o'er her face;
Where thoughts serenely sweet express
How pure, how dear their dwelling place.
And on that cheek, and o'er that brow
So soft, so calm, yet eloquent, T
he smiles that win, the tints that glow,
But tell of days in goodness spent,
A mind at peace with all below,
A heart whose love is innocent!

LAMB

Always the playboy poet, Jack.

JACQUELINE

That was beautiful. Did you write it?

JACK

Unfortunately, I'm better with the sword than
the pen. No, the author was Lord Byron.
Jacqueline, it was a pleasure meeting you. John,

always an adventure seeing you. Have a great night, both of you.

JACQUELINE

Good night, Jack. It was a pleasure meeting you too.

LAMB

See you, Jack. And for God's sake, have some fun. You are so damn serious all the time.

Lamb leads Aubrey away, while Tremeuse watches them go.

JACQUELINE

What's his story, John?

LAMB

I really don't know him that well. He's in the polo club and, man, is he an animal out there.

JACQUELINE

I wonder why?

LAMB

His father ran their family business for years. 200 hundred-year-old company. About fifteen, twenty years ago, your father bought it. Ugly scene. Hostile takeover. It was too much for the old man and he shot himself.

JACQUELINE

Shot himself?

LAMB

Rumor has it that Jack and his brother found the body.

Jacqueline is visibly shaken here. This is news she was kept from.

JACQUELINE

I didn't know that.

LAMB

It's no one's fault, just one of the unfortunate tragedies of business. The whole story is a Greek tragedy. Somehow they wound up with owner-ship in one of the largest gold mines in the world. Talk about a cruel twist of fate.

JACQUELINE

That's horrible. What happened to his brother?

LAMB

He's the assistant district attorney.

JACQUELINE

My God, this is so bizarre.

LAMB

It is. In fact, that's his brother over there. Roger Tremeuse.

JACQUELINE

Who's he with?

LAMB

That's Martha Dunn, his fiancée. From the Bal-
timore Dunns. Old money. Family is in insur-
ance. Good blood.

Camera pans to show Roger Tremeuse and Martha Dunn
chatting

LAMB (cont'd)

The brothers are complete opposites. Roger is
solid, steady, while Jack's a playboy.

JACQUELINE

He didn't act like a playboy.

LAMB

And he's attracted to you.

JACQUELINE

And I'm engaged to you.

LAMB

I know his type. Likes to win. You'd be a very
nice trophy on his arm.

JACQUELINE

So you're telling me that he would target me,
just to beat you.

LAMB

Yes.

JACQUELINE

I didn't get that impression at all.

LAMB

Forget Jack Tremeuse. We have a party to enjoy. Let's dance.

Lamb leads Aubrey out to the dance floor.

FAVRAUX MANSION

Different part of the room. The imagery is the same, but we are focused on Jack Tremeuse, Roger Tremeuse and MARTHA DUNN. All three are just beginning a conversation and have a drink in their hand. Jack has just walked over. He kisses Dunn and hugs his brother.

JACK

I don't think I've seen either of you since your engagement party.

MARTHA

And I don't think I've ever seen you without a date.

JACK

Actually, I have one here somewhere. She's pissed I lost her at the Opera. Surprised to bump into you both at Favraux's party.

ROGER

Politics create strange bedfellows. The mayor "requested" that the DA and I attend with him. Wants to get us in a show of solidarity.

Walking past this small group is Jenny Cocantin. Roger looks at her and she at him, their eyes meeting. Is there something there? Is there nothing? The audience does not know, but we do have something, we have a look of raw passion.

COCANTIN

Counselor...

ROGER

Detective. Allow me to introduce my fiancée, Martha Dunn and my brother Jack Tremeuse. This is Detective Jenny Cocantin.

MARTHA

Do you work with Roger?

COCANTIN

Not as close as we should, but our cases often cross.

JACK

I'm sure.

COCANTIN

Anyway, it's late and I was only crashing the party.

ROGER

Good night, Jenny.

COCANTIN

Good night.

Cocantin walks away and Roger is back to where he was.

MARTHA

Are you having a good time, Jack? I worry that you need a steady girlfriend, rather than seven different ones each week.

JACK

I'm actually having a great time.

MARTHA

Really?

JACK

Do you know Jacqueline Aubrey?

ROGER

That sounds vaguely familiar.

JACK

Delightful creature. I just met her a few moments ago. Her father is Favraux.

ROGER

Favraux?

MARTHA

If I didn't know better, Jack, I would say you had a crush.

JACK

I thought I knew everything about Favraux there was to know. How did I miss her?

ROGER

Just be careful, Jack. She is Favraux's daughter.
And I didn't know he had one.

Tremeuse looks at his watch. We focus on that shot and
read 10:15 p.m. He then looks about as if he has to be
somewhere.

JACK

I have to run folks. An early meeting and a late
night rendezvous to escape to.

ROGER

Always the dog, Jack, always the dog. And stay
away from Favraux's daughter. Nothing good
can come from it.

POLICE STATION INT. NIGHT

Sitting on a bench, smoking a cigarette is a disheveled
detective. He has been up all night and now has to pass
some news along that he knows will not be taken well.
His name is DETECTIVE DONALD KINAHAN. Walking up to him is the man from the District Attorney's
office. It is Roger Tremeuse. He is tired.

ROGER

It's four in the morning, detective.

KINAHAN

Hey Roger, sorry to get you out of bed so late.

Kinahan stands to greet Roger. The two men shake
hands as they walk down the hallway, a walk they have

taken a million times before. But somehow, this time will be a walk that neither forgets.

                    ROGER
That's all right, Donny. What's up?

                    KINAHAN
I've got men who will tell you that Santa Claus and the Easter Bunny don't exist, but they swear they saw a super hero last night.

                    ROGER
You lost me. A super hero? A man with what...powers? What do you have?

                    KINAHAN
Nothing. Something. Hell, I don't know. I deal in facts. But now, I have facts that add up to nothing.

                    ROGER
Why not start at the beginning and fill me in.

                    KINAHAN
Roger, This is so screwed I don't know where to begin. From out of nowhere he comes. We have reports from all over the city that this guy in a mask and costume, hit all sorts of illegal activities. It seems he only focused on the bad guys.

                    ROGER
The bad guys?

KINAHAN

Yup. If you were minding your business, then this character could give two craps about you. But if you were breaking the law, Jesus Christ, did he pay attention you.

Entering the room is a man that also looks like he has been up all night. A cigarette dangles from his lips as he reaches into his jacket to remove a pad and pen. He is a reporter that still does his job "old school." His name is PHILLIP GUERANDE.

GUERANDE

Assistant District Attorney Tremeuse and Detective Kinahan, would you care to comment on the recent attacks by a man in a mask?

ROGER

Who are you?

GUERANDE

Phillip Guerande, *Philadelphia Times*. I'm new to the paper, but now have the crime beat. Your cousin hired me.

ROGER

I'm sure. Tell Randolph, I owe him one.

GUERANDE

So, any comment on the masked avenger?

KINAHAN

No comment.

GUERANDE

In the last two nights, a masked vigilante has been reported. He has physically attacked dozens of men, destroyed hundreds of thousands of dollars of properties all tied to crime.

ROGER

Supposedly tied. There is no proof of any of this.

GUERANDE

No, proof? There is proof all over the city. It looks like a war zone out there. I understand you have a victim in the next room. Will you let him comment once released.

ROGER

If we have someone, that is his right.

KINAHAN

And he is not a victim, he's a suspect. Interview over, excuse us.

Both men enter the room and leave Guerande alone, who simply smiles.

POLICE STATION INT. INTERROGATION ROOM

It is closed and lonely. A single table sits in the center of the room. At the table is a man handcuffed to it. His face is beaten, he is tired and wants to be anywhere but there. He is a street punk. His name is KEN CARROLL.

Roger Tremeuse walks with Kinahan into an observation room. He wants to hear from those that actually witnessed the hero's debut, what they saw.

KINAHAN
(lighting up a cigarette)
I'm Detective Kinahan, this is Roger Tremeuse
from the District Attorney's office. We're going
to ask you some questions.

ROGER
Start from the top. What happened?

CARROLL
We was just looking for a little fun, that's all.
But that bastard in the mask had to hurt every-
one!

ALLEYWAY
Flashback Earlier that night. The scene is a dark alleyway. In the street are Carroll and an equally bad friend.
They are holding a woman, VICTIM, in a non friendly
way. A sole alley cat meows her anger at being disturbed
from mouse hunting.

CARROLL (V.O.)
We met this babe. She wanted to party and
y'know, who am I to say no?

KINAHAN (V.O.)
Yeah. You're a friggin' saint. What happened?

The two bad guys are starting to assault the victim. One
is holding her, while Carroll starts to unbuckle his pants.

CARROLL (V.O.)

Y'know, foreplay, some kissing. She got hot when I dropped my pants. Real Hot. Know what I mean?

POLICE STATION INTERROGATION ROOM

KINAHAN

Quit jerking us off. When did the mask arrive?

CARROLL

I can't think man.

Kinahan flies out of the chair and grabs Carroll by the lapel. He goes nose to nose with him.

KINAHAN

Well you better think, 'cause we're losing patience with you.

ALLEYWAY

The two bad men and the victim all freeze. From somewhere in the distance, a roar is heard.

CARROLL (V.O.)

It was like a wild beast man all over the alley. And then I saw this blur.

Into their midst drops a figure in black. Judex. He is on them in a flash. Fists flying, bodies dropping. We see this in the shadows.

KINAHAN (V.O.)

Did it talk? What did it say?

POLICE STATION - INTERROGATION ROOM
We are in a tight two shot of Carroll and Kinahan. If Kinahan could breathe fire, he would. He is snarling and spit is flying from his lips he is so worked up.

KINAHAN
What did it say?!

ALLEYWAY
The ground is littered with garbage and the bodies of the evil men. The victim is off to the side, not sure what has happened, but she is safe. The figure in black has Carroll in his arms, his body over his, pulling him in. The camera slowly zooms in until it is a close two shot of Judex and Carroll.

JUDEX
The innocent are protected by Judex.

Judex drops a gavel on the ground beside Carroll.

POLICE STATION - INTERROGATION ROOM
Carroll is being led away and Roger Tremeuse and Kinahan are still sitting in disbelief.

KINAHAN
I told you it was bad. It's worse. We've got a freakin' nut.

Tremeuse does not say anything; he is sitting, shaking his head while looking out.

KINAHAN (cont'd)
Who does this guy think he is?

Roger watches Kinahan look at the lights outside the window that represent man's accomplishments, seeing only victims waiting to be victimized.

                    ROGER
         He not only thinks that he is beyond the law, he
         thinks that he is the law.

Kinahan pauses, looking out again. He has one last thing to say and has not said it yet. He lights a cigarette, draws in on it, looks at the smoke, drops it to the ground. He snubs it out.

                    KINAHAN
         I gotta quit this, it's killing me.

                    ROGER
         Out with it Donny. What haven't you told me?

                    KINAHAN
         We're missing perps, Roger.

                    ROGER
         What?

                    KINAHAN
         They're missing. Vanished. I think that this
         Judex has taken them.

                    ROGER
         Taken them?

KINAHAN

Yeah. But it gets even funnier. From what we
can tell, the only ones he has taken are those that
have escaped the law.

ROGER

You lost me...

KINAHAN

You know that case the jury came back with
yesterday you tried?

ROGER

Yes. Archie Hinton. Someone screwed with the
evidence and once again that scum bag walks
free.

KINAHAN

Not anymore. He's missing too. And so is the
Judge.

EXT. PHILADELPHIA

Not a great part of town, very dilapidated and dirty. The
brash frankness of the poverty here should overwhelm
the setting. Not a great part of town. We see a rundown
building.

It is a boarding house. The sounds of the inner city are
prevalent in the background. People, horns, sirens in the
distance.

INT. FLOP HOUSE - NIGHT

Sitting on a bed in a dimly lit room, is Cal Hullen.
Somehow, this ex-con on parole has a pistol and he is

cleaning it. He sits in his pants and a sleeveless under-shirt. There is a sound across the room and the light goes out, causing Hullen to look up. Hullen is suspicious and takes out his gun as he looks about the room.

From in the shadows a dark hand comes, reaching Hullen and easily taking the gun from him. Judex is before him, but the audience only sees him from behind. A large hat covers his face.

            HULLEN
    Who are you? I don't have any money if that's
    what you want.

            JUDEX
    I am Judex, Mr. Hullen.

            HULLEN
    Judex? What do you want from me?

            JUDEX
    I want to offer you a job.

            HULLEN
    You have a funny way of asking.

            JUDEX
    Mr. Hullen, our stories are so similar we could
    be brothers.

            HULLEN
    So? That and a buck won't buy coffee these
    days.

                    JUDEX
You just spent years in prison, framed for a
crime by Favraux. You want revenge against
this man who ruined your life. In fact, you sat
here today planning how to kill him. Would you
say that I know who you are?

Hullen's eyes rage with horror and passion. Judex has
struck a nerve.

                    HULLEN
        What's your offer?

Judex in the shadows, smiles at him.

EXT. CITY STREET – DAY
Busy, bustling city street. A large skyscraper rises from
ground to 70 stories; it houses the Favraux office on the
23rd floor. Is the same building from the opening scene.

INT. SKYSCRAPER – CONTINUOUS
Elevator door opens, two generic OFFICE WORKERS,
Favraux, Monti and Morales step onto elevator. One per-
son pushes the button for the 10th floor.

                   WORKER 1
        What's on the 6th floor?

                   WORKER 2
        I don't know.

                   WORKER 1
        It's locked out.

                    WORKER 2
Press 6.

                    WORKER 1
I have. It's locked out.

                    WORKER 2
Someone likes their privacy.

The elevator stops passes the 6th floor. The one worker
shrugs his shoulders. The elevator stops at the 10th floor,
they step off. Favraux and his ladies continue up.

FAVRAUX'S OFFICE INT. DAYTIME
Favraux is sitting at the desk; with him are Monti and
Morales as usual. Sitting before him is Cocantin, his de-
tective.

                    COCANTIN
        It's not much Mr. Favraux, but I did learn a few
        things.

Favraux sits silently listening. He knows when to speak
and when to listen. He has a cigar in his hand, rolling it
unlit between his fingers as Cocantin speaks. Occasion-
ally, he sniffs it, taking in its aroma.

                    COCANTIN (cont'd)
        Aside from calling you at your party, this Judex
        visited a lot of your operations. Busted them up
        pretty good. And here is the kicker. Everyone
        that you paid us to have get off, he took.

FAVRAUX

Took?

COCANTIN

I mean they're gone. Vanished. No bodies, nothing. He took them.

FAVRAUX

He took who? I am not an unintelligent man detective, but I am not following you.

COCANTIN

Your people. People on your payroll that were arrested. People that you paid good money for us to taint evidence, to do whatever it took to clear them. He has. He took.

FAVRAUX

Why?

COCANTIN

I don't know why.

FAVRAUX

Stay on this, Cocantin. He has threatened my life, making a promise to me, one I intend not to see him keep.

COCANTIN

Can I ask what it was?

FAVRAUX

If I don't give a good amount of my fortune to a charity of his choice, he will kill me.

COCANTIN
(she looks confused by this)
Money? You're telling me that this whole thing
is about money?

FAVRAUX
Isn't everything?

COCANTIN
That just doesn't add up. He left all the money at
each of your places. He played hero to the rescue. It doesn't make any sense for this to be
about money.

FAVRAUX
Then, detective, I suggest you find out what it is
about and quickly.

Cocantin gets up out of her chair to leave. Favraux nods
to Monti, who hands Cocantin an envelope filled with
cash. She accepts it with a nod, places it in her purse and
prepares to leave the room.

FAVRAUX (cont'd)
Detective...

Cocantin stops at the door and turns to look at Favraux.

FAVRAUX (cont'd)
Do not let me down.

Cocantin opens the door and goes out.

FAVRAUX (cont'd)
Now, is everything set with Lamb?

MONTI
He and your daughter spoke at length of their upcoming wedding. She also spent a lot of time talking to Tremeuse.

FAVRAUX
He is nothing, just like his father. Is Lamb getting his visit today?

MONTI
Yes. They should be arriving about now.

DISSOLVE TO:

LAMB CONWELL OFFICE EXT VIEW
Downtown Philadelphia. Beautiful office building. Slow view up the building, then get closer on a window.

LAMB CONWELL OFFICE
Int. Shot of the offices of Lamb Conwell. It is immaculate, well designed. A RECEPTIONIST sits at the desk as Lamb comes around the corner.

LAMB
I have a visitor?

RECEPTIONIST
Yes Mr. Lamb. They are in the conference room.

Lamb walks into the conference room. Sitting at the table are two men. Both well dressed. They are from the

SEC. One is CLARK WEST and the other is BRUCE REEVES.

                    LAMB
I'm John Lamb. You wanted to see me?

                    WEST
              (handing over a business card)
Mr. Lamb, I'm Clark West, this is Bruce Reeves. We are with the Securities and Exchange Commission.

                    LAMB
What does this have to do with me?

                    WEST
Your personal trading record has come to our attention. We believe that irregularities have transpired with your activities.

                    LAMB
Irregularities? Are you kidding me? Do you know who I am?

                    REEVES
We know who you are Mr. Lamb. This is no joke. I have here a court order that will freeze all your personal assets until this matter is cleared.

                    LAMB
You can't do that.

> REEVES
>
> We will try to clear this up as quickly as possible Mr. Lamb, but right now our priority is getting to the truth.

> WEST
>
> You do want to get to the truth don't you?

> LAMB
>
> I want you to get the hell out of here.

Reeves places the court order on the large conference table in front of Lamb. Both men leave.

Lamb sits at the head of the table, his head down. He was just dealt a serious blow and has to think through this one. Yesterday he was on top of the world, today, he just had all his money taken from him. He has an idea and reaches for the phone.

> LAMB (cont'd)
>
> Get me Favraux on the line...NOW!

EXT. SKYSCRAPER – CONTINUOUS
Shot of 6th floor. Darkened windows.

INT. ELEVATOR – CONTINUOUS
From the first person view, a person enters a freight elevator from a loading dock in the back of the building. The person is in the shadows, a hat covering their face as they enter. The elevator stops at the 6th floor.

INT. JUDEX SECRET HEADQUARTERS
Hallway of prison cell.

Judex walks out of the elevator on the 6th floor. We see the hat and jacket on the floor. He walks past a series of jail cells. Several disheveled characters, who are imprisoned against their will, scream to be released.

Judex walks along the corridor looking into each cell. From within the cells, we hear men and women shouting for release. Judex ignores their cries. He moves slowly through, until a man meets him. This is Cal Hullen, a man that owes his life to Judex. He serves as jailer. Hullen ignores the prisoners and greets the person Judex.

> HULLEN
> You were busy last night, Judex.

> JUDEX
> This is the beginning Cal. They escaped justice once. They won't escape it twice.

> HULLEN
> We have to talk.

> JUDEX
> What's on your mind?

> HULLEN
> I visited the doctor yesterday. You have to find someone else to manage this prison.

> JUDEX
> But our job is just beginning. We still have Favraux out there.

HULLEN

It's not that I don't want to or don't have the
heart for it
    (Beat)
...actually, it is exactly that. I don't have the
heart for it.

JUDEX

We are not inhumane to them.

HULLEN

You don't understand. My heart...it's no good. It
can go at any time.

Judex places his hands on Hullen's shoulders.

JUDEX

I had no idea.

HULLEN

I want to live each day, continue our mission,
but you need to find someone else to watch over
them.

JUDEX

Whatever you need...

HULLEN

Favraux. I want to see Favraux in here before I
die.

EXT. PHILADELPHIA STREET

A black stretch limousine is driving down the streets.

INT. LIMOUSINE

Two shot from the front to the back seat. Favraux is in the middle, Morales to the right side by the window. Favraux is sitting with his arm about the shoulders of Morales.

> ### FAVRAUX
> We will need to step up security around the mansion.

> ### MORALES
> We already have extra men coming in.

> ### FAVRAUX
> Good. I feel comforted already. Have we identified who we are missing?

> ### MORALES
> The list is long. All our people. Cocantin was right.

> ### FAVRAUX
> Who is this Goddamn Judex?

> ### MORALES
> We're working on that.

> ### FAVRAUX
> Send Reeves and West a bonus. Lamb after today's meeting should be humbled and...
> > (closes eyes in pleasure for a moment)
> ...that's it...
> > (Beat)
> ...and all ours.

Monti sits up from the left side, creating a three shot from the two shot, and smiles at Favraux then kisses him and then kisses Morales.

MONTI

Everything is under control, baby. We are not going to let anything happen to you.

Favraux smiles widely and puts his other arm about Monti.

INT. JAIL

Cal Hullen opens the cell of Archie Hinton. Hinton sits on the edge of his bed in a straightjacket and with shackles on his feet.

HINTON

What you want?

HULLEN

Come with me.

HINTON

I ain't going nowhere til you tell me what's goin' on.

HULLEN

You're in jail.

HINTON

What jail? I ain't even been arrested. The judge set me free.

                    HULLEN
So he did.

                    HINTON
I got rights.

                    HULLEN
Sure you do.

INT. INTERROGATION ROOM INSIDE OF JUDEX's JAIL

The scene is viewed from monitors by Hullen. As we watch it, he is recording it. But as he watches it, the view shifts to show us body temperature, blood pressure, etc.

Hullen brings Hinton inside the room and has him sit. Judex lays out a case on the table. He opens the bag and Hinton sees a variety of tools and needles.

                    HINTON
Who are you?

                    JUDEX
Judex.

                    HINTON
What...what's that? Judex?

                    JUDEX
You could say, I'm the jailer.

                    HINTON
What jailer?

                        90

JUDEX

Your jailer.

HINTON

Get the hell outta here. What do you want with me?

JUDEX

You're here because Justice needs to be served.

HINTON

I want my lawyer.

JUDEX

You still believe you are in their world Mr. Hinton. You're not. You're in my world. And in a moment you will be in a world of pain.

HINTON

What you gonna do to me?

Judex begins taking out an alcohol swap and wiping down Hinton's arm. Hinton looks at him in shock and disbelief.

HINTON (cont'd)

What are you doing?

JUDEX

Mr. Hinton, I want you to tell me a story. This will help make sure you tell me the true story.

HINTON

I don't know nothing...

JUDEX
Everybody knows something Mr. Hinton. Even you.

HINTON
I ain't saying nothin' until I get a lawyer.

Judex walks to his case, picks up a long sharp needle. He then walks back over to a bound and struggling Hinton, who he then injects. Then, with dramatic flair, walks back to his bag where he takes out a long silver pin. It glistens in the cell.

HINTON (cont'd)
What...what are you doing...?

JUDEX
Mr. Hinton...let's talk about pain. You have caused a lot of it over the years. I want to know all about it.

Cut to black. A loud scream from Hinton.

INT. LAMB'S OFFICE – CONFERENCE ROOM
Lamb is sitting and the Receptionist opens the door, leading Favraux in with Morales and Monti. Favraux takes the seat to the right of Lamb.

FAVRAUX
You asked to meet with me...?

LAMB

Do you have any idea what happened to me today?

FAVRAUX

You have gotten sloppy and lazy and as a result
our dealings are in jeopardy.

LAMB

You knew what was happening?! And you
didn't do a Goddamn thing!?

Lamb stands up. He is mad and getting very angry.

FAVRAUX

Sit down.

LAMB

I will not! Listen to me fat man...

Morales is in motion quickly. She reaches for Lamb,
uses a martial arts move to take him down and has him
on the ground, a knife appearing out of nowhere at his
throat.

FAVRAUX

No. You listen to me. This nonsense with the
government will go away after you return from
your honeymoon. But your interest in this firm
will transfer to me.

LAMB

It was you. You set me up.

FAVRAUX

No. You did this yourself. I am simply cleaning
up your mess.

LAMB

You son of a...

FAVRAUX

If I was the bastard you think I am, I would not
allow you to marry my daughter. Your business
will continue, but my brains will be upon your
shoulders.

LAMB

I can't believe this is happening...

FAVRAUX

And, should you take your frustrations against
me out upon my daughter, there is no imaginable
pain to describe the hell I will call down upon
you.

Morales does something with Lamb's arm and shoulder
causing Lamb to scream out in pain.

FAVRAUX (cont'd)

Good day John. I will see you tonight at your
engagement party. Be in good spirits.

Favraux, Monti and Morales walk out of the room, while
Lamb stays sitting on the ground, looking up with ha-
tred.

INT. JUDEX SECRET HEADQUARTERS

Judex walks out of the cell with Archie Hinton in it. Hullen is waiting outside.

JUDEX

Archie Hinton had quite a story to tell. Perhaps our next stop will fill in the gaps.

Judex enters into a jail cell. Sitting in disbelief is Judge Wexler.

JUDGE WEXLER

Where am I?

JUDEX

You are here Judge Wexler, because you failed her. You broke her heart.

JUDGE WEXLER

Failed her? What are you talking about?

JUDEX

Justice. Lady Justice. You failed her when you betrayed her.

JUDGE WEXLER

You're insane. Do you know who I am?

JUDEX

Judge Herman Wexler. Harvard Law School class of 1970. Not top of your class and thanks to two other students not the bottom of your class either. But no case was too big...especially if there was a pay day to you.

JUDGE WEXLER
What do you want from me? I want to go home.

JUDEX
I want to know about your master, Judge Wexler. I want to know about Favraux.

JUDGE WEXLER
I have nothing to say.

We see Judex take out his case with the tools and needles. Wexler's eyes open in fear.

JUDEX
Let's see about that, shall we?

EXT. FAVRAUX ESTATE
Sitting outside at a table overlooking the massive backyard is Jacqueline Aubrey and her best friend, GENEVIEVE DiSIMONE. They have drinks before them as they sit and chat. Both are casually attired. Jacqueline more sedated than Genevieve, in cargo pants and a relaxed top. Genevieve is dressed to the nines.

GENEVIEVE
Have you and John decided on your honeymoon?

JACQUELINE
Not yet Genevieve. It happened so suddenly and I wasn't sure if John was who I wanted to spend the rest of my life with.

GENEVIEVE

You mean aside from traveling the world with an exciting man?

JACQUELINE

My father is successful. My son and I want for nothing, yet, I feel as if this is something that my father almost arranged.

GENEVIEVE

Arranged? Where do we live, in Medieval Europe?

JACQUELINE

That's not what I mean. John and my father work together. You saw them both here the other night, they are almost inseparable.

GENEVIEVE

Like your father and those two women?

JACQUELINE

I don't even want to discuss that one. And then, well, I met someone I can't stop thinking about.

GENEVIEVE

Now we're getting somewhere. Who?

JACQUELINE

Jack Tremeuse.

GENEVIEVE

The Jack Tremeuse? He's left a trail of broken hearts behind him. The one date wonder.

JACQUELINE
He was captivating, almost mesmerizing and he
did something that I've never seen done.

GENEVIEVE
What's that?

JACQUELINE
He didn't back down to Daddy or John.

GENEVIEVE
That's because he doesn't need their money.
Good looks and more money than God. That's a
combination I find hard to resist.

Both ladies start to laugh.

JACQUELINE
Well behave, because I invited him over for
lunch.

GENEVIEVE
You didn't?

JACQUELINE
I did. He should be here shortly.

A young boy run into the scene now. He is Jacqueline's
son, CHARLIE. He runs up to his mom. He is in soccer
practice clothes.

CHARLIE
Hi mom, hi Aunt Genevieve.

JACQUELINE
Hi honey. How was practice?

CHARLIE
Great. We have our first game Saturday.

GENEVIEVE
I like the shorts, Charlie... they make you look sexy.

JACQUELINE
Go inside and get some lunch.

Charlie runs inside to eat.

JACQUELINE (cont'd)
(laughing)
You are too much sometimes.

GENEVIEVE
He'll thank me when he's older and remember I taught him how to be cool with chicks.
(Beat)
Now...Why did you call Jack Tremeuse?

INT. DISTRICT ATTORNEY'S OFFICE
Sitting at a desk is the District Attorney, WILLIAM EISNER. He is a man older than Roger Tremeuse. Standing before him is Roger. He is here to tell a sane man, something insane. On the DA's desk is a gavel that he keeps touching.

EISNER

Sweet Jesus, are they sure?

ROGER

Are they sure that some creature in a mask dropped from the roof of a building and beat dozens of men?

EISNER

Find this thing. Work with Kinahan and set up a task force if you have to, but make your number one priority finding this...this...what does he call himself?

ROGER

Judex.

EISNER

Jesus Christ. Judex. Just what I need.

ROGER

It would appear that he is on our side.

EISNER

Our side! We have no side. All we want is to find this Judex and get him behind bars.

ROGER

I meant the side of justice. That is what I thought we were after.

EISNER

Justice, Roger. Let me tell you about justice. It's a cruel mistress that will always leave you. Now,

I've got to go and tell the Mayor that he has someone in Philadelphia who is pissed at more than the Goddamn Phillies.

EXT. FAVRAUX ESTATE
Backyard patio with table. Jacqueline Aubrey is sitting outside with her girl friend, Genevieve DiSimone. THE BUTLER arrives with Jack Tremeuse behind him.

BUTLER
Mr. Tremeuse, Madam.

JACQUELINE
Thank you.

Jack Tremeuse walks over to shake Jacqueline's extend hand.

JACK
It was a pleasant surprise to get your invitation today, Jacqueline.

JACQUELINE
I hoped it wasn't presumptuous, but I thought since we had such a lovely chat last night, why wait?

JACK
Why wait?

JACQUELINE
Jack Tremeuse, this is Genevieve DiSimone.

JACK
Genevieve, my pleasure.

GENEVIEVE
Don't get formal on my account, I'm just leaving.

Genevieve bends over to kiss Jacqueline on the cheek.

GENEVIEVE (cont'd)
I'll talk to you later honey. It was nice meeting
you Jack... and I can find my own way out.

Jack sits down in the seat vacated by Genevieve.

JACK
I have seen her before, somewhere.

JACQUELINE
Genevieve is the principal lead with the Pennsylvania Ballet. I'm surprised you two haven't
met before. She seems like your type.

JACK
And what type would that be?

JACQUELINE
A fun gal.

JACK
And you're not fun?

102

JACQUELINE
(laughing)
Probably not the type you're used to.

JACK
If you were, I wouldn't be here.

JACQUELINE
Would you like something to drink?

JACK
I'll have what you're having, thank you.

JACQUELINE
John tells me you were quite the football player in high school. Said both you and your brother could have gone pro.

JACK
Maybe. Didn't seem that important to me.

JACQUELINE
What about your brother...John mentioned that he was recruited by every big time program and he goes to Penn. Turns down the NFL for law school.

JACK
Your fiancée is good. Trivia buff?

JACQUELINE
I don't think so. I googled you. You turned everybody down for scholarships also. Can I ask why?

JACK

Went to see the world. I really wasn't dependent on college to get a job with my family's fortune waiting, so I bummed around a bit. Europe, Asia, where ever the breeze took me.

JACQUELINE

Why did you come today?

JACK

I could ask you why you invited me, but I'll be a gentleman and answer your question. I came because you asked. I came, because, I wanted to see you again.

JACQUELINE

Are you always this direct, Jack?

JACK

Only when asked a direct question. Can I ask you a question?

JACQUELINE

That only seems fair.

JACK

Why did you call me?

JACQUELINE

Jack... What happened between you and my father?

JACK

I should be going now. Thank you for the invitation. I enjoyed seeing you again.

JACQUELINE

Jack... Don't go. Not yet.

Jack stands up, his back to Jacqueline. He is looking out across her yard at the wonders and the beauty there. He never looks back at her.

JACK

Jacqueline...I know I am being too forward in my words, but I find in you a woman that I can't get out of my mind. But, there is a history at work here. He's your father and this is his house and I will not speak against him. Especially not here. Thanks for the lunch invitation, but I should be going now. Good bye.

Jack walks away while Jacqueline looks on in wonder and awe.

FAVRAUX ESTATE - INT. BEDROOM EARLY EVENING.

It is a large magnificent bedroom. We are coming in at the end of Favraux and the Valkyries' lovemaking. Once done, Favraux is dressing in a tuxedo while, sitting on the bed in their sexy undergarments, are Monti and Morales. They are also finishing getting dressed, but they are putting weapons in secret holsters above their stockings.

Favraux is sitting at a table while the ladies are dressing. Three short glasses with a sugar cubes on spoons above the glasses are before him. Pouring from a bottle of Pernod, he pours an inch into the bottom of each of the glasses over the sugar cube with absinthe.

He then lights the sugar cubes on fire. As the short flame dances and drips into the glasses, he then pours ice water over top, bringing the glasses to half full. He drops the sugar cubes into each glass, and, with the spoon, stirs the green liquor into the water, turning it into a cloudy haze. Each lady reaches for their glass after the process is done which takes place during the dialog that follows.

FAVRAUX
The dinner to celebrate my daughter's engagement starts shortly.

MORALES
You're not worried are you, baby?

FAVRAUX
With my two Valkyries at my side? Never.
(pause)
However, should anything happen to me, I want you to give this to my daughter.

Favraux removes an envelope from his pocket and places it on the dresser. It is addressed to Jacqueline.

FAVRAUX (cont'd)
Do you understand my wishes?

MONTI

No one will get close enough to you to hurt you, baby...

FAVRAUX

But should something happen to me, this goes to Jacqueline.

Favraux smiles as he looks at both women. His cell phone rings. No one has this number. It is a call only phone and this is the second time in 24 hours it has had an unknown number.

JUDEX (V.O.)

Favraux...

FAVRAUX

You are a little early, Mr. Judex.

JUDEX (V.O.)

What did you decide?

FAVRAUX

I think my money will stay where it is, thank you.

JUDEX (V.O.)

Then I have a gift for you. In your dresser is a DVD player. In it is a movie just for you. Simply turn it on and press play.

FAVRAUX

How the Hell did...?

JUDEX (V.O.)
Ask me at eight tonight.

Favraux shuts the phone off in disgust. Monti and Morales know the stakes just went up. They all look at each
other and drink their drinks.

Favraux walks to his dresser and finds the DVD player
just as Judex promised. He lifts the lid, and pushes play.

MOVIE ON THE DVD PLAYER
We see Judex before images of Favraux. He obviously
filmed it with a green screen to give off no clues of
where he is. This is the first time we get a clear view of
his appearance.

JUDEX
Mr. Favraux. We meet at last. Forgive me for
not doing this in person, but I have much to do
in anticipation of our meeting tonight.

Behind Judex are scenes from Favraux's life. Business,
play, things that are seen by many, things that only
Favraux would see. The point being made by Judex is
that he has been where he should or could not have been.

JUDEX (cont'd)
You have been busy since your rise to power.
Some make money the honest way through hard
work, but others prefer the old fashion way, by
stealing it from others. You fall into the later.
But don't take my word for it. I have many of
your associates here with me, wishing to tell a
story. Your story. So grab some popcorn, pull up

a chair and enjoy the flicks. And make sure your two lovelies are watching, they are part of the story.

The images cuts to the cells holding many people that Favraux had in his control. Finally, we end with a view of Judge Wexler. He is in his cell and is not a happy camper.

JUDGE WEXLER

For fifteen years I have served the wishes of Richard Favraux. Cases would come before me, cases that he wanted to go one way or another, and I would see to it that they did.

(jump in time)

The first one was a man thirteen years ago named Hullen. Favraux wanted him out of the way. He took over his business when he bought a company in a hostile takeover, forced Hullen into an action that he knew would have dire consequences, and I put the nail in the coffin with my sentence. I have never forgot the way Hullen looked at me when he was taken out of the court room.

(jump in time)

How? Oh...I started working for Favraux when I got into debt. His bank was not going to loan me anymore money and all other banks dried up on me. The one day I was summoned to his office. My debts would be paid, but I had to provide a service. I sold my soul to the devil.

INT PRIVATE GYM

Working out and totally fit and buff are Jack and Roger Tremeuse. Their muscular, extremely well toned and defined bodies glisten with sweat as they go through repetition after repetition. As they work out, they chat.

JACK

What about the rumors of a "superhero" making citizen arrest in the city last night. Any truth?

ROGER

It's insane. We have a nut in a costume, dropping from the sky to fight crime. Not a superhero. Jesus, if the press heard that. And he's not content with fighting crime like a comic book superhero should.

JACK

Is he faster than a locomotive? Does he leap tall buildings in a single bound?

ROGER

That's faster than a speeding bullet, more powerful than a locomotive, by the way and I don't think so.

JACK

So what's his story?

ROGER

He likes to collect things.

JACK

What things?

ROGER

Criminal things. He takes his prey and I'll be damned if I know where.

JACK

You're serious. A vigilante? What does our esteemed District Attorney think of all this?

ROGER

Not much. It's an election year and this isn't going to help. He read me the riot act for suggesting that this vigilante at least seemed to have his priorities straight. The mayor and DA are in an uproar. I just want to go back to being a mild-mannered DA.

JACK

You are anything but mild-mannered Roger. I guess this big a story could hurt them both...especially if you run for office.

ROGER

Still deciding if I will or not. Your turn. What's new with the company?

JACK

Are you asking as my loving, curious brother or are you asking as the second largest shareholder?

ROGER

Both.

JACK

I'm in DC all day tomorrow with Tremeuse Defense. Some hush-hush government project. They have me and two other firms with ultra high security clearance in for some crazy discussions.

ROGER

Do we know what firms we're competing with?

JACK

Wayne and Stark.

ROGER

About what?

JACK

I'm not sure. It sounded like a defense plan, but the tone of the representative sounded more like an offensive device. But, I'll cover all that during the board meeting next month. Will you be there?

ROGER

Of course. You know at times you remind me of that character in *Atlas Shrugged*.

JACK

Which one?

ROGER

Francisco d'Anconia.

JACK

How so?

ROGER

He said that it was the goal of every d'Anconia heir to expand the family empire by at least ten percent. Since Pop died...

JACK

Killed himself.

ROGER

Killed himself, and you decided to recreate the company, you have increased its original profitability over hundred percent in the last ten years.

JACK

Are you complaining that you are now a billionaire rather than a mere millionaire?

ROGER

Not at all. My point is that I thought you were nuts when we were kids. Not going to school here. Going to Japan, Germany, Switzerland. Studying martial arts and history. Now it makes sense. Where all our ancestors were happy just making guns, you recreated Tremeuse Arms into Tremeuse Defense, outsell Favraux and become defense system supplier to governments all over the world. Pop would have been proud.

JACK

Sometimes I wonder Roger. Sometimes I wonder.

FAVRAUX MANSION – INT. DINING ROOM

The table is set beautifully. Lamb is there beside Jacqueline, and Favraux is at the head. On the right and left of him are Monti and Morales. TWO OTHER COUPLES are sitting. Genevieve DiSimone is there with a DATE.

Jacqueline does not look overly happy, but not sad either. She is confused. There are random shots of the guests talking, eating and drinking, all designed to show us that time is elapsing. Favraux taps his spoon on his glass to call attention to his guests that he wishes to say something. He rises.

FAVRAUX

I would like to thank you all for coming tonight. This is a special evening, one that gives me pride and joy.

From around the table are various agreements and patting of the back.

FAVRAUX (cont'd)

My daughter is the light of my life and is a beautiful woman. John is one of my most trusted and valued friends, and a greater union could not exist.

We hear a clock begin to toll slowly, loudly. Favraux looks across the room and sees (in a cutaway) the clock is turning to eight p.m. A grin crosses his lips as he sees the time.

FAVRAUX (cont'd)

So my friends, I ask you to rise and join me in a
toast to the happy couple.

Everyone at the table rises and lifts their glasses.

FAVRAUX (cont'd)

Long life...

ALL

Long life!

Favraux sips his champagne then coughs. He looks
about in shock and bewilderment. He coughs again then
grabs at his chest and throat. His eyes bulge and he drops
to his seat, a look of shock on his face. Monti and Morales are by his side but he slips down out of the chair,
falling to the ground.

He is dead.

The clock ends tolling. It is eight. Jacqueline screams in
horror as Lamb holds her, his eyes on Favraux's body.
The room is in shock.

INT. POLICE COMMISSIONERS OFFICE

Police Commissioner ROBIN KIRBY is in shock. Nothing could have prepared her for the horror loose in her
city. She is sitting at her desk when Detective Kinahan
walks in.

KINAHAN

You wanted to see me Commissioner?

KIRBY

Sit down Kinahan.

She pulls a bottle out from under her desk and pours two whiskeys, passing one to the Detective. He shakes his head 'no thanks' and she smiles before draining hers.

KIRBY (cont'd)

Lieutenant... Donny... do you mind if I call you Donny, we have a situation. A bad situation.

KINAHAN

Yes. I've seen what he can do first hand.

KIRBY

And your take is...

KINAHAN

I'm not sure yet.

She looks at him, wondering what he means. Slowly, she reaches for the glass she poured him and drinks that one.

KIRBY

Why?

KINAHAN

Part of me, the part that is a cop, knows that this is wrong. But Jesus Christ, he has them in fear. The criminals and the animals that pretend to be men are afraid. Part of me likes that. Can you understand what I am trying to say?

KIRBY

Yes. Now understand what I am trying to say. Find him. Arrest him. Shoot him dead in the street resisting arrest if you have to. I want you to head a task force and bring me this bastard's mask on a platter.

EXT. CEMETERY

Standing alone at a grave site is Jacqueline Aubrey. John Lamb is near her. Monti and Morales are still there, now watching their master's daughter. Cars are leaving as the bystanders realize she wants to be alone.

TREMEUSE OFFICES INT VIEW

Sitting at his desk is Jack Tremeuse. A computer is working behind him and he is just finishing a call. He places the phone down and his intercom rings.

JACK

Yes, Susan?

INTERCOM VOICE

Jack, a Mrs. Aubrey is here to see you.

JACK

Really?... Send her in.

The door opens and the secretary, Susan, leads Jacqueline Aubrey into Jack Tremeuse's office.

JACQUELINE

Thank you.

JACK

This is a surprise.

JACQUELINE

I had to get out of the house, Jack. I hope you don't mind my coming here.

JACK

Not at all. I was just getting ready for tea, can I offer you some?

JACQUELINE

Tea would be wonderful.

Jack gets up from behind his desk and walks over to an area that is set up for a Japanese tea ceremony. The water is boiled and Jack is beginning to pour. While he is preparing the tea and pouring for Jacqueline, he is speaking. The camera captures shots of both during this process, his preparing, her interest in what he is doing.

JACK

The custom of drinking tea dates back to China before the 9th century. By the 16th century, in Japan, Sen no Rikyu, who is perhaps the most well-known historical figure in the tea ceremony, introduced the concept of *ichi-go ichi-e*, which means literally "one time, one meeting." This is a belief that each meeting should be treasured, for it can never be reproduced.

JACQUELINE

You spent a lot of time in Japan I see.

Jack sits down in a chair near her, so that they can talk while sipping their tea.

                    JACK
Quite a bit.

                    JACQUELINE
Do you miss it?

                    JACK
It is part of me. As is Europe.

                    JACQUELINE
You do have a fascinating history.

                    JACK
Not really, just old. Enough of me, how are you making out, Jacqueline?

                    JACQUELINE
This is the first time that I have just sat since my father died.

                    JACK
I've been meaning to talk to you about that, Jacqueline.

                    JACQUELINE
I now know a little of the tragic history between our families.

                    JACK
Jacqueline...

                    JACQUELINE
Jack, that's not why I came here. I just had to get
out of the house. It seems that everyone wants a
part of me, now that Daddy left me his estate.

                       JACK
I don't want to lose a friendship with you. There
is so much from the past it poisons the future.

Jacqueline reaches across the chairs to put her hand on
Jack's hand.

                    JACQUELINE
We have time. There is no rush. I'm just glad to
have gotten to know you.

Jack looks at his hand, with her hand over it. He looks
up at her. Their eyes meet as he covers her hand with
his.

                       JACK
C'mon, let's get out of here.

                                          CUT TO:

INT. RESTAURANT
Jack and Jacqueline walk her arm in his. It is an extremely fancy restaurant. A well dressed man comes to
greet them. His name is LOUIS FEUILLADE.

                     FEUILLADE
Jack, a pleasant surprise.

JACK

Hi Louis. This is a spontaneous decision. I hope
you can seat us, you look pretty busy tonight.

FEUILLADE

Our pleasure to have you join us again. A table
for you and the lady?

JACK

Louis Feuillade, this is Jacqueline Aubrey. Louis
owns this dive.

FEUILLADE

Ah, Ms. Aubrey, I am charmed to meet you.

JACQUELINE

Thank you.

FEUILLADE

And my condolences on the loss of your father.

JACQUELINE

Thank you.

FEUILLADE

Please, follow me.

Feuillade leads the pair to a private dining area. It is an
out of the way table. They sit down.

JACQUELINE

Sounds like you come here often.

JACK

I love French cooking and this is the best anywhere. Including Paris.

JACQUELINE

That's a big boast. Any recommendations?

JACK

To be honest with you, I never order from the
menu.

JACQUELINE

You don't?

JACK

Nope. Just let the chef do what he wants to do.

JACQUELINE

Then I'll have the same.

INT POLICE STATION

Sitting at their desks are Kinahan and Cocantin. Both are
working on their computers when Cocantin pops over.

COCANTIN

Any headway on that Judex mess?

KINAHAN

Not much. People are still missing, no clues and
the Commissioner wants results.

COCANTIN

That sucks. If I can help, let me know.

KINAHAN

Thanks Jenny, but I'm working it pretty hard with Roger.

COCANTIN

I've noticed him.

KINAHAN

He's hard to miss.

COCANTIN

I don't get him.

KINAHAN

Whatta you mean?

COCANTIN

He's worth all that money. And yet he's spending his time as an Assistant District Attorney.

KINAHAN

With his popularity, he could be the next DA. And then who knows. He's young enough, could be mayor, governor, senator...maybe president. That takes money, and he's got that.

COCANTIN

Yes he does.

INT. RESTAURANT

Jack and Jacqueline are finishing up their meal. An empty bottle of wine is before them, plates finished up.

                    JACQUELINE
That was unbelievable.

                       JACK
It always is. Listen, the night is young, and I really don't want it to end.

                    JACQUELINE
Me either.

                       JACK
A night cap?

                    JACQUELINE
Let's. Any suggestions?

                       JACK
I have a 1947 Cheval Blanc I had been saving
for a special occasion. I think that would be perfect right now.

They look at each other.

                                        CUT TO:

<u>TREMEUSE ESTATE</u>
The main living room is grand, huge in scale. Jack and
Jacqueline are on the couch, a fire roaring near them as
they sip their drinks.

                       JACK
Jacqueline...

JACQUELINE

No words.

JACK

I... I have to talk to you... I have to tell something...

JACQUELINE

Jack, not now. Not now.

Jacqueline melts in Jack's arms, as they kiss. She unbuttons his shirt and feels the power in his chest. The new lovers get lost in the passion of learning of each other by firelight.

The storm outside bellows in the distance.

INT. BEAUTIFUL HOME IN THE COUNTRY
Sitting at a breakfast table is Roger Tremeuse, his mother, Ann Tremeuse, and Martha Dunn.

ROGER

Mom, I'm glad you had a chance to join us.

ANN

You know I have a hard time coming to Philadelphia since your father died.

ROGER

I know. But the city is as beautiful as ever. And the restaurants and culture are thriving, making it an American Paris. You really should have let me take you out for dinner last night.

ANN

Is it true?

ROGER

Is what true, Mom?

ANN

That when Favraux died he dropped dead in our old house? The home of generations of Tremeuse?

ROGER

Mom...

ANN

I just want an answer. Yes or no.

ROGER

Yes. He did.

ANN

I hope your father and all your ancestors watched as that bastard dropped dead.

ROGER

Mom, there has to be something else we can talk about.

ANN

Had you been to the house lately?

ROGER

Martha and I were there with Jack for a fund raiser the night before Favraux died.

ANN

I hope you put poison in his wine.

ROGER

I am the assistant district attorney of Philadelphia. Justice must be served, not vigilantism.

MARTHA

We do have a vigilante in Philadelphia. A masked avenger that is called Judex.

ANN

That's well and good but I waited for years for revenge on that man. He betrayed your father's trust, stole the family home before your father's last investment paid off, tossed us into the streets.

ROGER

It all worked out mom. We got the diamond mines and it worked out. Jack rebuilt a company just like Pop's and it is one of the largest in the world. Larger than Favraux's.

ANN

How is Jack?

MARTHA

Handsome as ever.

ANN

But is he happy?

MARTHA

He looks it, but you can't tell. Did Roger tell
you, he is thinking of running for District Attorney next year? He'll make a great DA.

ANN

As long as he understands that criminals must be
punished.

ROGER

The guilty must be punished Mom. That's why
we have courts. So every man or woman gets a
fair trial, judged by a jury of their peers. Any
other way and the system fails and we have an-
archy.

INT. BEDROOM OF JACK TREMEUSE - MORNING
Jack is asleep in bed. Jacqueline gets out and dresses
quietly. She then bends over, kisses a sleeping Jack and
leaves.

As she leaves, unknown to her, Jack's eyes open, his
ears listening to her every move.

RANDOM SHOTS OF THE CITY
The new day is beginning. Deliveries are being made,
people are going to work.

INT. FAVRAUX ESTATE.
The living room. Jacqueline is sitting, at her desk, trying
to get a handle on the massive estate that she inherited,
last night with Jack, and what she has to do.

Lamb brings over a drink to her. She smiles and accepts it. Into the room steps the butler.

                    BUTLER
          Miss Aubrey... Misses Monti and Morales are
          here to see you.

                    JACQUELINE
          Show them in please.

The two mistresses of her father enter the room. Both are also in black, but look like two angels of death. Sexy and dangerous. They walk over, kiss her and stand before her.

                    MONTI
          Jacqueline, we have something for you.

                    JACQUELINE
          That's alright... you were important to my father
          and I appreciate your friendship with him, but I
          don't need any gifts.

                    MORALES
          It's not a gift. This is from your father.

                    MONTI
          To be given to you in the event that he died the
          other night.

Jacqueline is in shock. How could this statement be?

                    JACQUELINE
          He knew...he suspected this would happen?

MORALES

The night of the party, a man threatened him.

MONTI

A man that calls himself, Judex.

MORALES

He told your father that he would die within twenty four hours unless he donated his fortune to charity.

JACQUELINE

Why didn't he go to the police?

MONTI

He did. In his way. Please, take this letter. Knowing your father, I am sure it explains everything.

Monti hands Jacqueline an envelope. Lamb looks on in bewilderment. This is another unexpected turn.

Monti, then Morales, walk over to Jacqueline and kiss her on one cheek; then the other lady kisses her other cheek. It is as if they are paying tribute to the heir of a czar. They turn to leave.

MORALES
(to Lamb)
Perhaps we should give her a moment alone, Mr. Lamb?

LAMB
(not really wanting to go)
Oh yes, of course.

Lamb, Morales and Monti leave the room.

Jacqueline opens the envelope. We watch as she reads the letter, in shock and sorrow. The words are private between her and her father.

INT. FAVRAUX ESTATE - OUTER ROOM
Morales, Monti and Lamb stand there.

LAMB
What the Hell happened to the fat man?

MORALES
If we find out you had anything to do with this, you are a dead man.

LAMB
You dare to threaten me? Here?

MONTI
There isn't any place we wouldn't go to kill you. Remember that.

Monti and Morales join hands and walk out the door, leaving Lamb behind to watch them.

INT. JUDEX SECRET HEADQUARTERS
Judex and Hullen are in the main room. They are over a body working on him. We cannot see the man on the table.

INT. FAVRAUX ESTATE - THE LIVING ROOM

Jacqueline is there with Lamb. She is at the piano tinkering as he comes up behind her. Her mind is idle, one finger then another brushing the keys, every so often playing a short melody. She is still in shock from the turn of events.

                    LAMB
A month in Europe and you'll feel much better.

                    JACQUELINE
I don't think so John. I think that I spent too much of my time feeling better.

                    LAMB
What does that mean?

                    JACQUELINE
I'm going to donate all this money.

                    LAMB
              (Upset and panicked)
What are you talking about?

                    JACQUELINE
I've done some checking. I must have been blind not to have known before. My father left a wake of destroyed people behind.

Lamb sits silently in shock listening to her speech. It is all happening too fast for him. First the money that was his being frozen, now his fiancée talking about donating away her money. His head is reeling.

She turns to look at him and stops playing with the piano.

> JACQUELINE (cont'd)
> There is no way I can know who was hurt so I could live a life of privilege, but I can try to make a difference on other levels. I am going to give it away.

> LAMB
> You want to give away our money?

> JACQUELINE
> Our money? You haven't married me yet. If you were only marrying me for my father's money, it will be gone soon.

> LAMB
> Jacqueline let's talk about this...
>> (Beat)
> Please be sensible...No one in their right mind just gives away one billion dollars.

> JACQUELINE
> I will. Just watch me.

Lamb turns and leaves.

Once alone, Aubrey collapses on the chair, exhausted. She mindlessly begins tinkering on the piano. It is a passionate piece that picks up intensity as it builds. The music is full of sorrow and heartbreak, building in intensity until she slams her fingers down on the keys to end it, then rides that emotion to continue playing. She plays the first fifty seconds of the work; her emotions, which she had to keep in check, all come out at the key board. Then she stops short, mid note... Her phone rings.

                    JACQUELINE (cont'd)
Hello?

                    FAVRAUX (V.O.)
Jacqueline... forgive me.

                    JACQUELINE
Daddy? DADDY!

INT. JUDEX SECRET HEADQUARTERS
Hullen is in the hallway in front of the cells. He is peering into one of the cells.

INT. JUDEX SECRET HEADQUARTERS INT CELL
Judex is standing there over a body asleep. The body is turned away from us, but as he wakes up, we see him. It is Favraux.

                    JUDEX
Welcome to your new home, Favraux.

                    FAVRAUX
          (he is very groggy, just coming out of
          his "sleep")
What the Hell...Where am I?

                    JUDEX
Your new home. Welcome.

FAVRAUX
You can't keep me here.

JUDEX
The outside world thinks you are dead.

FAVRAUX
You're insane.

JUDEX
Probably, but I am now your jailer.

Judex walks to the cell door and speaks through the opening.

JUDEX (cont'd)
Come in, please.

Into the room walks Hullen. Favraux sees him and once his mind makes the association, he reacts.

JUDEX (cont'd)
I see you recognize the man that will watch over you.

Camera focuses on Hullen here.

JUDEX (V.O.) (cont'd)
Do you remember Cal Hullen? You came in swiftly and stole what little his family had be-cause you wanted the land. But to get it, you had to ruin him, bankrupt his family and take the land. So, you made him offer to get the land back.

Favraux is upset. He is disoriented and this is too much. We are back to a wide shot with Judex, Hullen, and Favraux.

> JUDEX (cont'd)
> And once he did your bidding, he had him framed and sent away.

> FAVRAUX
> This is wrong.

> JUDEX
> Your tossed away rubbish becomes my treasure.

Camera focuses on Hullen in this shot.

> JUDEX (V.O.) (cont'd)
> You had to humiliate him. Take away all that was his. Disgrace him. So you set him up to take the fall for some of your shady deals.

We are back to the group shot.

> FAVRAUX
> This isn't right. You can't do this. There are laws to protect me.

In the background, we can and should have been hearing the screams of those that are locked away without hope.

JUDEX

Laws that you made a mockery of. Laws that you twisted and corrupted. Well, Justice is blind no longer.

Favraux looks in disbelief. Judex takes a phone out from beneath his robes. He presses a button and hands it to Favraux. Hullen removes a pistol and holds it to Favraux's head.

JUDEX (cont'd)

You may ask your daughter to forgive you.

Close Up on Favraux.

FAVRAUX

Jacqueline...
        (Beat)
...forgive me.

In a two shot, Judex takes the phone, disconnects the call and puts it away.

INT. THE POLICE STATION

We are in a small room. It is very busy. Kinahan is sitting at his desk and across from him, Cocantin is at hers.

Roger Tremeuse enters the room.He locks eyes with Cocantin, then he nods to Kinahan, who gets up to join him.

They walk into the interrogation room to chat.

INT. POLICE STATION
INT. INTERROGATION ROOM

Kinahan and Roger Tremeuse sit at a table. Roger has a cup of coffee, Kinahan a cigarette. They are both tired and wanted someplace private to chat.

KINAHAN

What do you make of Favraux dropping dead?

ROGER

Somehow I know this all connected.

KINAHAN

I've always suspected he was tied up in something dirty, but he keeps himself so clean playing with that blue blood set...no offense.

ROGER

None taken. The DA wants us to find out what the Hell is going on.

KINAHAN

So does the Commissioner.
          (Beat)
Roger, I have my nose to the grind stone. I am talking to every scum bag that crawled out from under a rock, but there is nothing on this Judex or Favraux.

ROGER

Stay on it, Donny. Let me know what I can do to help.

KINAHAN

I will... Roger, would you mind if I ask you something?

ROGER

Sure, anything.

KINAHAN

Favraux and your family...bad blood, wasn't there?

ROGER

Do you think I killed him?

KINAHAN

Hell, no. I was just wondering if you could be objective with this, that's all.

INT. POLICE STATION
EXT. INTERROGATION ROOM, THE ANTEROOM
Watching the above conversation in the interrogation room on a computer monitor is Cocantin.

INT. JUDEX SECRET HEADQUARTERS
INT. FAVRAUX'S CELL.
Sitting on the cot is Favraux. His door opens up and Hullen walks in. He tosses a bundled brown paper wrapped package tied with string at him.

FAVRAUX

What's this?

HULLEN

You're in court today.

Favraux looks at him in shock.

INT. JUDEX SECRET HEADQUARTERS

A courtroom. The time is unknown. Hullen leads a man-
acled Favraux into the room, then secures him in a chair.
Various monitors line the room. On one monitor we see
a young couple, David and Betsey Gaines. On another
monitor is a woman, Ann Tremeuse. They obviously are
using web cams to watch the proceedings. Walking in
and sitting at a podium before them is Judex.

> JUDEX
> This court is now in session. Who stands ac-
> cused before this court first?

> HULLEN
> Archie Hinton your honor.

> JUDEX
> And what is he accused of?

> HULLEN
> Murder.

> JUDEX
> And who accuses him?

> DAVID GAINES (O.S.)
> We do. David and Betsey Gaines. That monster,
> Archie Hinton, killed our son.

> JUDEX
> Bring in the defendant.

Hullen walks out of the "court room" and returns a few moments later with a bound man. This is Archie Hinton. He is large and mad. For days he has been locked up against his will. Once Hinton is secured, Hullen steps out... during the following he will return, leading Judge Wexler into the courtroom.

                    JUDEX (cont'd)
You have been accused of murder. How do you plead?

                    HINTON
This ain't no court.

                    JUDEX
This is a court of the people that doesn't allow corrupt officers of the law to destroy evidence. This is where the guilty are punished. Now...what did this man do?

                    BETSEY GAINES (O.S.)
He killed our son when he turned evidence and was going to testify that he accidently saw him commit another murder.

                    JUDEX
And was he convicted in a court of law?

                    DAVID GAINES (O.S.)
The evidence was tainted. When the case came to trial, it was missing. The case was thrown out and our son lies dead in the ground.

JUDEX
Who tainted the evidence?

DAVID GAINES
Someone with a lot of pull had the evidence destroyed.

JUDEX
Someone such as Mr. Favraux who is here?
Speak Favraux. You traded a life for a life. Was this man worth it?

FAVRAUX
You can't prove anything. This is a kangaroo court.

JUDEX
Indeed. But I beg to differ. Judge Wexler, how say you...what happened to the evidence?

JUDGE WEXLER
A detective arranged for it to be played with.

JUDEX
What detective?

JUDGE WEXLER
Cocantin. We both work...worked for Favraux.

FAVRAUX
Shut your mouth Wexler. Not another word.

JUDEX
Does the truth scare you, Favraux?

FAVRAUX

This isn't a court... this is a mockery.

JUDEX

What you created in the outside world was a
mockery. A mockery of justice. A mockery of
humanity. A mockery of life. This is where we
correct such mistakes and allow justice to be
served.

FAVRAUX

You call this...THIS...justice?

JUDEX

The truth they say will set you free Judge
Wexler. Do you feel freer now?

JUDGE WEXLER

No. I want to be released.

JUDEX

And I want Justice for those that have been op-
pressed and wronged by men like you that were
sworn to uphold laws. The court sentences
Archie Hinton to life behind bars with the sentence to begin immediately. The court also sentences Judge Wexler to the same fate for his betrayal of the trust placed in him by society.

Wexler sinks to his seat as Hullen drags a fighting mad
Hinton out of the court room. The Gaines log off.

JUDEX (cont'd)
This brings us to you Mr. Favraux.

Favraux stays in his seat, his arms folded. He will have no part of this "court" and will not make it easy for them.

JUDEX (cont'd)
Of what crime is this man accused?

HULLEN
Murder. Kidnapping. Arson. Embezzlement. Theft. Conspiracy.

JUDEX
How do you plead?

FAVRAUX
I don't plead anyway as I don't recognize your power over me.

JUDEX
Who accuses this man?

Ann Tremeuse speaks through the monitor.

ANN
I accuse him.

JUDEX
Who are you to accuse this man?

ANN
I am Ann Tremeuse. A widow that he created.

JUDEX
And of what do you accuse this man, Favraux?

ANN
This man stole my family's business, ruined my husband and forced him to kill himself. I ask the court for his death.

This statement gets Favraux's attention. He knows that he is kept in the cell against his wishes, but no one has spoken of death before.

FAVRAUX
You're mad. You wouldn't dare kill me.

JUDEX
Keep a civil tongue in your head, Favraux. There is nothing that we would not dare to do to you. You are not in the world anymore.

ANN
I demand you find this man guilty and put him to death.

JUDEX
That is a very serious wish.

ANN
This man deserves death.

JUDEX

That might be so, but a higher court than this one is the only one that can make that judgment you request. Life behind bars without parole. Court dismissed.

Hullen drags a struggling Favraux out.

ANN

That man deserves death.

JUDEX

We must not become what we fight against.

ANN

Favraux will find a way to free himself and when he does, he will kill you.

JUDEX

I can't kill a man in cold blood. No matter what he did, I can't do that.

ANN

As long as he breathes, his victims are not avenged.

Ann Tremeuse logs off. Judex stares at the blank screen in silence.

INT. THE VELVET ROSE.

A very nice upscale bar. The bar is full of beautiful people. Lamb is sitting at the bar having a drink. He is upset and mad. He does not notice when Cocantin walks in. Every other man does.

COCANTIN
Wallowing in pity, John?

LAMB
Screw you.

COCANTIN
Not with that attitude.

LAMB
I wasn't sure you were coming.

COCANTIN
You said you had something important to talk about. Does it relate to your lost fortune?

LAMB
You heard about that?

COCANTIN
Of course I heard about that.

Lamb signals to the BARTENDER. She walks over to them.

LAMB
Another Johnny Walker Black rocks. I don't know what the lady is having though.

COCANTIN
The lady is having a French martini, and keep the vermouth away from my glass please.

BARTENDER

Coming right up.

Shot of bartender making the drinks. The liquor cabinet is all glass and lit up. Multi colors illuminate the bottles. She reaches for the two bottles and brings them down. She then makes the drinks.

LAMB (O.S.)

Here's the deal. We need to get my former fiancée to give us some of that fortune.

COCANTIN (O.S.)

She's not going to just give it us. I hear she gave you your walking papers.

LAMB (O.S.)

That's right. But that doesn't mean she can't be persuaded.

COCANTIN (O.S.)

You think?

Shot on Lamb in the foreground with Cocantin in background. He has heard her comment and knows that it is incorrect.

LAMB

I know her. Her soft spot is her son, Charlie. She'd do...or pay anything to protect her son.

COCANTIN

What are you saying?

LAMB

I say we take the boy and let her pay to get him back.

COCANTIN

That's insane. I'm a cop...a detective.

LAMB

You were on Favraux's payroll for years. You're as dirty as they come. Don't try to play coy with me.

The bartender comes over with the drinks and places them down.

COCANTIN

Taking some evidence, giving him some information, big deal. No one got hurt. You're talking about kidnapping. I won't do it.

LAMB

You will do it. I have records of all your dealings with Favraux. Not only will you go to jail, but your pension is gone, your reputation, no more rich married sugar daddies, nothing. It all goes away.

COCANTIN

You son of a bitch. How dare you!

LAMB

Shut up. You'll come out of this fine...and with some serious coin in your pocket. I'm not greedy. 60/40 split on two million will take you far, detective.

COCANTIN
Then we need her to make a donation to us.

EXT. SOCCER FIELD
A game is being played between two groups of ten year old boys. In the crowd is Jacqueline Aubrey, Genevieve DiSimone and various other people. She is with the folks rooting for the team in blue. On the field among the blue uniforms is Charlie.

EXT. SOCCER FIELD
PARKING LOT NEAR SOCCER FIELD.
Inside a car sitting are Lamb and Cocantin. They are watching the crowd from the distance. A second car pulls up. Inside are two men, PETER SHAFFERY and SCOTT PRICE. They talk to the first car.

SHAFFERY
We're here. Which one do you want grabbed?

LAMB
Charlie Aubrey. He has on number one in the blue jersey.

SHAFFERY
You got the money?

Cocantin tosses an envelope into the car window. Shaffery looks at it and frowns.

SHAFFERY (cont'd)
This ain't all of it.

COCANTIN
You don't have the kid yet.

PRICE
Then we're square.

COCANTIN
After this job, we're done.

Cocantin tosses a package into the car also.

SHAFFERY
What's this?

COCANTIN
Wear it when you do the job.

The car with Shaffery and Price drives off.

INT. JUDEX'S SECRET HEADQUARTERS
FAVRAUX'S CELL.
Judex and Favraux are within the cell.

FAVRAUX
They'll be looking for me Judex.

JUDEX
You are wrong Favraux. I can keep you here for as long as I please. Everyone thinks you are dead.

FAVRAUX

But my daughter...you had me call her. And I am a figure in the public eye... There will be questions and an autopsy to determine how I died.

JUDEX

You could be right. But you are not.

INT. FAVRAUX'S MANSION
FLASHBACK. THE DINING ROOM.

Favraux is laying on the floor in the dining room. Monti and Morales are over him, Lamb has Jacqueline in his arms.

An ambulance crew arrives to take him away. Three men are part of the crew. Judex in disguise with Hullen, all with makeup on to cover up their identities. They come in with the stretcher and bend over to go to work on Favraux.

HULLEN

Please give us room.

Judex is injecting Favraux, "trying" to revive him. Hullen prepares the stretcher.

JUDEX

I'm getting no response. We have to get him to the hospital.

JACQUELINE

Please, save my father. Don't let him die.

Judex's head turns at these words. Perhaps it is this wish from her that allows him to spare her father—who can know?—but his eyes lock with hers. When he realizes he is looking too long, he turns away.

JUDEX
We'll do our best.

The ambulance crew gets the stretcher under Favraux and wheels him out. Outside, they get him into the ambulance. Monti starts to climb in but Hullen stops her.

HULLEN
You can't ride with us.

Hullen closes the door, while Judex sits with Favraux in the back. Hullen then walks to the front to drive to the hospital.

INT. AMBULANCE
Judex is over Favraux. He is still unconscious. Judex takes out a cell phone.

JUDEX
This is Judex. We are on our way. And we will have company. Be ready.

INT. JUDEX'S SECRET HEADQUARTERS
FAVRAUX'S CELL
Judex and Favraux are continuing their conversation.

JUDEX
At the hospital, the doctor, a man that owes me the life you tried to destroy, pronounced you

dead. Then the coroner, another man in my service, found that you died of a massive coronary. A street person that died that same night now lays in a casket that your money paid for beneath a tombstone that prays that you rest in peace.

Favraux sinks down on the bed as the severity of his situation becomes clear.

FAVRAUX
But how...how did you get the poison in me?

INT FAVRAUX HOME - BEDROOM
Favraux is asleep with the two Valkyries on either side of him. A figure in the shadows enters the room and stands over the sleeping bodies. A fine spray mist is sprayed over the bodies. Then Judex takes out a syringe and we

FADE OUT.

EXT. SOCCER FIELD. SOCCER GAME LATE AFTERNOON.
The game is over. The two teams are leaving. Jacqueline is giving Charlie a hug. She and Genevieve are standing side by side.

JACQUELINE
That game was amazing... you guys are awesome!

CHARLIE
Thanks Mom! I'm going to ride my bike home, okay?

                    JACQUELINE
No stops on the way?

                     CHARLIE
One if I can have ice cream money…

Jacqueline reaches into her purse to take out a five dollar
bill. She hands it to her son. He takes it and stuffs it in
his sock.

                    JACQUELINE
One stop, then right home.

Charley gets on his bike. He puts on his helmet on and
take off. Genevieve puts her arm in Jacqueline's as they
walk off.

                     GENEVIEVE
        I'll meet you at your place. A good chardonnay
        would hit the spot right about now. Too many
        yummy soccer dads.

In the distance we see the boy riding off. A car slowly
tracks them, following them. It is Shaffery and Price. No
one notices.

INT. GIORDANIO'S OFFICE - NIGHT TIME
Sitting around the room are all the men that Favraux had
aligned to himself earlier, minus Lamb and Cocantin.
These include Giordanio, Holland, Foreman, and Zhou.
Giordanio seems to have called the meeting. It is near
the end.

GIORDANIO

I think we need to continue the organization the way that Favraux set up.

ZHOU

You do?

GIORDANIO

Things worked pretty well when there was a singular head on the organization.

ZHOU

And who would you suggest that be?

GIORDANIO

What I am suggesting is that we focus on what he brought to the table and see how we can do that together.

HOLLAND

But we also took some big hits, when his enemies came.

ZHOU

And where is Lamb? And that cop?

GIORDANIO

They didn't answer my calls.

HOLLAND

They could be part of whatever happened.

The doorway opens. Favraux's Valkyries are there, looking as hot and deadly as ever. The security guards move over to intercept them. It fails and they have their asses kicked. At their feet lay the men.

GIORDANIO

It's not easy to replace men these days. You could have knocked.

MONTI

I thought we did.

GIORDANIO

You weren't invited.

MORALES

That's not polite.

HOLLAND

We want to know where Lamb and that cop are.

MONTI

They, Mr. Holland, are plotting and conspiring. They are using each other.

GIORDANIO

For what purpose?

MONTI

To get Favraux's fortune.

FOREMAN

Maybe we should figure out a way to get our hands on that.

MONTI

From this moment forth, you will work for us. We will guide your organizations as Mr. Favraux did.

MORALES

Any objections?

Around the room the people look at each other but no one says anything.

EXT. FAVRAUX MANSION - MID AFTERNOON. BACK PATIO.

Present are Jacqueline and Genevieve. They have a bottle of wine open and are sitting outside enjoying it.

GENEVIEVE

Are you sure you want to give all this up?

JACQUELINE

I am not giving all this up. That wouldn't be fair to Charlie. But I am donating the bulk of my father's estate.

GENEVIEVE

I don't know about that. You have a life and a life style that people would kill for.

JACQUELINE

Genevieve, there is so much good I can do with this money. You have to understand that. It's...

Jacqueline's cell phone goes off. Like her father, her number is not known by many.

JACQUELINE (cont'd)

Hello?

MUFFLED VOICE (O.S.)

Mrs. Aubrey?

JACQUELINE

Yes…

MUFFLED VOICE (O.S.)

Charlie would like to say hello.

JACQUELINE

Charlie?

CHARLIE'S VOICE (O.S.)

Mom!! They have me...

JACQUELINE

CHARLIE!!!!

MUFFLED VOICE (O.S.)

This is Judex. I have your son. No harm will come to him.

JACQUELINE

What do you want? Anything, please! Don't hurt my baby!

Genevieve looks on in shock as her friend pleads on the telephone.

MUFFLED VOICE (O.S.)

We want two million dollars in cash. You will be called. No police. We will be watching you. One wrong move and it is over for Charlie. Are we understood?

JACQUELINE

Yes.

MUFFLED VOICE (O.S.)

If we are not pleased with your actions, in four hours we will send him back in bite size pieces. Will you have the money?

JACQUELINE

Yes. I'll get the money.

INT. RESTAURANT

Sitting at a table are the Tremeuse brothers, Jack and Roger.

ROGER

We don't seem to be able to get together very often it seems.

JACK

I know. My schedule lately has been hell. How's City Hall?

ROGER

Aside from the Judex and Favraux crap, fine. The fat bastard drops dead, and his name is across my desk more now than when he was alive. Then I have this vigilante that seems to have a hard on for Favraux.

                    JACK
Why are you telling me this?

                    ROGER
You wouldn't know anything about this masked avenger would you?

                    JACK
What does it matter? Favraux is dead.

                    ROGER
It matters because we have laws.

                    JACK
Well the only laws I care about are the ladies and the steak I'm about to order. I'm starving

                    ROGER
This isn't over Jack.

Jack's cell phone rings. He answers it.

                    JACK
Jack Tremeuse.

                    JACQUELINE (V.O.)
Jack...

                    JACK
Jacqueline?

                    JACQUELINE
I didn't know who else to call...who else to
trust...

                    JACK
Slow down...What's wrong Jacqueline?

                    JACQUELINE (V.O.)
It's my son. He's been kidnapped by Judex.

                    JACK
    What?!?

Jack is out of his seat in a flash.

                    JACK (cont'd)
    I have to go.

Roger Tremeuse looks in curious wonder at his brother
as he races out of the building.

INT. FAVRAUX MANSION
Jacqueline and Genevieve are still in shock, with Genevieve comforting Jacqueline. Jack Tremeuse comes into
the room silently.

                    GENEVIEVE
    How the Hell did you get in here? I never heard
    you come in.

                    JACK
    What happened?

GENEVIEVE

We were at her son's soccer game. Then we came here, and Judex called. He wants two million dollars.

JACK

You are sure it's Judex?

JACQUELINE

He said he was. And this Judex killed my father, so why not take my son!

JACK

Jacqueline...I promise you, we will get your son back.

JACQUELINE

They should be calling any minute now. What do I do?

JACK

Act natural.

JACQUELINE

But they have my son...

The cell phone rings. All heads turn to look at it on the table. Jacqueline reaches for it. Jack puts his hand over hers, and with the other, places his hand gently on her cheek.

JACK

Remember, you want to listen and agree. When we know what they want, we can create a plan.

Jacqueline nods in agreement and picks up the phone.

> JACQUELINE
>
> Hello…

> MUFFLED VOICE (O.S.)
>
> You didn't answer quickly. Did you contact the police?

> JACQUELINE
>
> I swear to God, I didn't.

> MUFFLED VOICE (O.S.)
>
> Did you tell anyone?

> JACQUELINE
>
> My friend was here when you called. She is still here and hasn't told anyone either. Please, I want my son back. What do you want me to do?

> MUFFLED VOICE (O.S.)
>
> You are sounding smarter. Stay smart and you might see your son by breakfast.

> JACQUELINE
>
> Anything.

> MUFFLED VOICE (O.S.)
>
> Bring the suitcases with the two mil to the water works.

> JACQUELINE
>
> By the Art Museum?

MUFFLED VOICE (O.S.)
Yes. Be there in one hour. Once we know you are alone, we will signal you. You give us the money and we will tell you where to pick up your son.

JACQUELINE
No.

MUFFLED VOICE (O.S.)
What did you say?

JACQUELINE
If I don't see my son, I won't give you the money.

MUFFLED VOICE (O.S.)
The water works in one hour.

The line goes dead. Jack looks her in the eyes.

JACK
You have the money?

JACQUELINE
Daddy always kept a lot here for emergencies.

JACK
(holding her hand)
You have to trust me.

JACQUELINE
I do.

JACK

Then do what they ask. I'll make sure you get your son back and your money.

JACQUELINE

I don't care about the money.

JACK

Jacqueline, if they get the money, the boy is as good as dead and so are you.

EXT. THE WATER WORKS - LATE AFTERNOON.

This is an old landmark in Philadelphia culture. A building that, at the turn of the last century, was the number one tourist spot in America, now is just sitting in Philadelphia, above the Schuylkill River, in the shadow of the Art Museum.

In the distance we see a guitar player and hear an acoustic guitar playing. The scene itself is empty, devoid of people except for the street musician playing. Through various shots, we find ourselves getting closer to the building as the camera comes in closer.

The car driven by Shaffery and Price pulls up. Shaffery gets out dressed in a pseudo Judex costume and surveys the surroundings. Momentarily, a second car pulls up. It is driven by Jacqueline. She gets out of the car. She looks around and sees "Judex." He holds up a hand to stop her.

SHAFFERY

That's far enough.

JACQUELINE
My son. Let me see him.

SHAFFERY
Take him out.

Price gets out of the car and has a strong grip on Charlie. He is still in his soccer uniform and has a look of fear in his eyes.

SHAFFERY (cont'd)
Okay, you've seen him. Show me the money.

Jacqueline opens her passenger car door and takes out two large suitcases. It is obvious that the cases are heavy.

Shaffery gives her the signal to walk forward a few steps. She does awkwardly. He looks around to see if anyone is watching. Price walks forward with Charlie a few steps also. Shaffery is still looking around.

While this is happening, our guitar player, who is forgotten about, should have the song morph into a violent concerto type thing. This bridge should be part of the song, so that to the audience, this transition is natural. The couple of steps forward by Jacqueline and then by Price continues until they meet in the center where Shaffery is waiting.

SHAFFERY (cont'd)
Open the cases.

Jacqueline kneels down to open the suitcase. She turns to the one on the left.

> SHAFFERY (cont'd)
> No. The other one.

She switches to the other one and opens that one. The case is open and the money is seen inside.

> SHAFFERY (cont'd)
> Okay. Now walk to my car.

> JACQUELINE
> You have the money. Let Charlie and me leave.

> SHAFFERY
> You know we can't do that.

Jacqueline wraps her arms around her son, covering him with her body. Her eyes are pleading with Shaffery and Price. Both are stone cold killers. That is why they were chosen by Favraux's corrupt detective.

Into their midst comes a black flash. From the direction of the guitar player comes Judex racing over, twin automatic pistols in his hands. He hits Price, spinning him around as he falls to the ground, having taken a shot that will eventually be fatal. Shaffery takes aim, but Judex rolls and comes flying into the fake Judex. The two enter into a death fight.

> JUDEX
> Get out of here!!

The Two "Judexes" continue to fight, with the battle ending with the real Judex landing a death blow on Shaffery.

Jacqueline grabs the boys and runs to her car. Shaffery lies dead on the ground as Judex stands over him, while Jacqueline and Charlie drive off. Price crawls slowly to his car, blood trailing behind him. Judex stands and watches.

EXT 5 STAR HOTEL
View looking at the hotel from outside to establish shot.

INT. HOTEL SUITE MASTER BED ROOM.
In it are Lamb and Cocantin. They are waiting for Shaffery and Price to arrive with the money. Both have drinks in their hands, and it is obvious that they have just concluded making love. They are in the bedroom, in a state of undress.

LAMB
One million dollars will go far.

COCANTIN
I suggest you stay low profile for a bit. No big spending.

The doorbell rings frantically downstairs. Lamb gets out of bed and throws a bathrobe on. Cocantin has a puzzled glaze on her face.

LAMB
Be right back.

Cocantin gets out of bed and quickly starts to get clothes on as she grabs her weapon.

INT. HOTEL SUITE MAIN FOYER
Lamb opens the front door. Price is holding his guts in with one hand, supporting himself in the door frame with the other.

LAMB
Jesus Christ, get in here.

Price stumbles in the room.

LAMB (cont'd)
What happened?

PRICE
Judex was there. He killed Shaffery. I don't know why I'm not dead.

Cocantin enters the room now, in her pants and black shirt, that she has not had time to tie, so her bra is exposed with her pistol out. She is all business. Fun time is over. There is no time for modesty.

COCANTIN
Because he wanted you to lead him to us.

She fires one bullet into Price, killing him on the spot. Lamb is in shock.

LAMB
Oh my god, you shot him.

COCANTIN

Shut up. Judex is coming, we have to leave.

LAMB
(Panicked)
What!?! Here!?! Oh God.

Cocantin throws Lamb a pistol. He catches it and looks at it as if it were on fire.

COCANTIN

If it moves, shoot it.

The two race out the back way, running down the hallway. From the shadows, Judex watches. Cocantin turns a corner, with Lamb behind her looking around. Judex aims a pistol at him and fires a dart into his back, dropping Lamb.

INT. POLICE STATION - WAITING AREA.
Benches line the wall. Detective Kinahan and Roger Tremeuse are sitting. Kinahan slowly inhales on his cigarette.

KINAHAN

You must hate when I call.

ROGER

Well, my curiosity sure rises. What's going on?

KINAGAN

We just got a tape from channel 2. They're breaking a story at six and wanted us to see it first. I thought you should see this.

                    ROGER
    Judex?

                    KINAHAN
    What else?

Kinahan gets up and walks to VCR. He pushes play.

ON THE SCREEN WE SEE:
Video tape of news report.

                    HOLLOWAY
        This is Penny Holloway for Channel 2 news. We
        have exclusive footage of a battle in our streets
        at the historic Water Works.

The camera leaves Holloway and now we have a video
camera, long distance shot footage at the water works of
the gun fight with Judex and the fake Judex.

                    HOLLOWAY (V.O.) (cont'd)
        A tourist at our historic Waterworks was lucky
        enough to hear gunshots and turned his camera
        on the scene. What we have is carnage and mur-
        der.

Pull back to show we now have a view of Holloway with
the microphone in her hand as she speaks.

                    HOLLOWAY (cont'd)
        From what we can gather, a kidnapping was
        foiled by Judex. Who were the victims? Why did
        he choose to interfere? What lets him think he is

above the law or that he replaces the law? These are questions that must be answered. This is Penny Holloway, reporting for Channel 2 news.

INT. POLICE STATION
Kinahan turns off the television.

KINAHAN
Well, there you have it.

ROGER
You want me to stop that broadcast?

KINAHAN
Yeah. We also have surveillance tapes from the building. It was Favraux's grandson kidnapped.

ROGER
This doesn't get better.

KINAHAN
You want more? I have one of the two perps from the gunfight dead in a suite at a 5 star hotel downtown. How the Hell does that happen?

ROGER
Let's go get a drink.

INT. FAVRAUX MANSION EVENING
Jacqueline is sitting in the living room with her son Charlie. Genevieve is still there. The room is silent; everyone is still pretty shaken up by the turn of events. The butler enters the room. He has the two suitcases that Jacqueline had brought with her.

BUTLER
Madam… these just arrived for you.

JACQUELINE
Where did they come from?

BUTLER
A messenger dropped them off. He handed me this note to give to you.

Butler hands Jacqueline an envelope. She opens it.

GENEVIEVE
What does it say?

JACQUELINE
That I am not your enemy.
(Beat)
It is from Judex.

INT. JUDEX HEADQUARTERS - EVENING
In the main office area is Hullen working. Judex enters with Lamb over his shoulder.

HULLEN
Another?

JUDEX
John Lamb. I think there is much he can tell us. What cell is open?

HULLEN
The one two down from Favraux.

174

Judex turns to walk out; Hullen follows.

INT. JUDEX SECRET HEADQUARTERS
LAMB'S CELL.
Lamb wakes up and finds himself in a cell. Judex is standing over him.

                    LAMB
          Where am I?

                    JUDEX
          Your new home, John Lamb.

                    LAMB
          No...no...This isn't my home.

                    JUDEX
          You kidnapped Charlie Aubrey. You served
          Richard Favraux for years to achieve your gains.
          They say No Pain, No Gain. Well, you had the
          gain, in here, you will have the pain.

                    LAMB
          NNNOOOOOOOOO!!!!

INT. JUDEX'S SECRET HEADQUARTERS
FAVRAUX'S CELL
Favraux is in his cell. All about him are images of his life, and he has no place to hide. Then it all stops.

Judex comes in with Hullen.

HULLEN

Your old associates are turning against you
Favraux.

FAVRAUX

If they think I am dead, how can they turn on
me?

JUDEX

They kidnapped your grandson.

FAVRAUX

Is he safe?

JUDEX

I got there in time.

FAVRAUX

Who took him?

JUDEX

Lamb and Cocantin.

FAVRAUX

I'll kill them.

JUDEX

You're days of revenge are over.

INT. PRIVATE CLUB - EVENING
Roger Tremeuse is sitting at a table with Detective
Kinahan. This is an extremely fancy club.

KINAHAN

The nuts here cost more than a beer at my local bar. So what do you make of all this?

ROGER

We have to get our hands on this Judex. No man is above the law and we can't allow a vigilante to terrorize the city.

KINAHAN

Favraux, dead as he may be, keeps coming up in this mess. What's your take on him?

ROGER

He was a corrupt business man that didn't care about anyone or anything and went from white collar crime to high stakes crime when no one was looking. Will he be missed? Not by me.

KINAHAN

What happened with him and your family?

ROGER

My father trusted him. He offered to expand our family business, a business that went back to the Revolutionary War, and wound up taking it.

KINAHAN

And your father committed suicide...

INT. TREMEUSE SENIOR OFFICE LOBBY

Flashback. This is a continuation of the opening scene in William Tremeuse's office.

The scene begins in the lobby down stairs. Two young boys are waiting for elevator. They are young Jack Tremeuse and young Roger Tremeuse. With them is their mother, Ann. The elevator opens people exit followed by Favraux. He sees the Tremeuse family.

FAVRAUX
Mrs. Tremeuse...boys.

ANN
Go to Hell, you son of a bitch.

FAVRAUX
This is a dog eat dog world, Mrs. Tremeuse.

The elevator door closes, and the Tremeuse family is behind it while it rises.

INT. TREMEUSE SENIOR OFFICE - MAIN OFFICE
William Tremeuse lies dead behind the desk, his chair knocked over backwards.

His son Jack followed by Roger run in. Jack screeches to a stop as he sees his father. While in shock, he turns to stop his brother. Coming in behind the boys is Ann Tremeuse. She sees her husband and the boys standing in shock and horror at the sight before them. She wraps her arms around the boys, her face a painting of pain. She knows that there is one man responsible for this.

INT. JUDEX SECRET HEADQUARTERS - MAIN CORRIDOR
Hullen is walking down it looking in on the prisoners. The sounds of agony fill the halls but he hears none of it.

He stops and looks in on John Lamb. Staring in a moment, Lamb looks up and sees Hullen. They talk through the bars.

                    LAMB
You look familiar.

                    HULLEN
I never traveled in your fancy circles Lamb.

                    LAMB
I know that voice...I know your voice.

                    HULLEN
We've never met.

                    LAMB
We have...I know we have.

Hullen opens the cell door and walks in. Lamb steps back then sits on his bed.

                    HULLEN
I see something in your eyes...something that reminds me of someone. Someone I lost a long time ago.

                    LAMB
I know who you are, but you can't be...you're dead.

                    HULLEN
Rudy...

LAMB
You're my father. You're Cal Hullen!

HULLEN
Rudy!

The two men embrace in the cell.

LAMB
They told me you died.

HULLEN
I was as good as dead. Favraux set me up for his crimes and I was sent away.

LAMB
Favraux? Why? You had nothing.

HULLEN
The man wanted everything, and that included what little we had.

LAMB
I didn't know.

HULLEN
But what happened to you? How did you become John Lamb?

LAMB
I was sent to foster home after foster home. I wanted to be anyone but who I was. This name served me.

HULLEN

But you served him.

LAMB

I didn't know. I didn't know what he did to you.
If he wasn't dead, I'd kill him.

HULLEN

There will be no killing. He isn't dead. He's
here.

LAMB

Here?

HULLEN

Yes.

LAMB

You work for Judex?

HULLEN

Yes.

LAMB

Why?

HULLEN

He offered me a second chance. Your mother
was dead, you vanished...I thought you were
dead too. I wanted to kill Favraux when I got
out. I spent every moment in the stinking cell
wanting to kill Favraux.

LAMB

Then why didn't you? Why did everyone tell me
you were dead?

HULLEN

I didn't want you know what I had become. I
was an animal that was put in a cage. No father
wants their child to see them that way.

LAMB

I'm so confused. I made decisions... did
things...thinking that you were dead...aligned
myself with...with Him.

HULLEN

It's not too late, Rudy. Judex, offered me a second chance at living. I can give that to you.

LAMB

Are you sure?

HULLEN

Come with me...

Hullen leads Lamb down a corridor. They get into an
elevator, where they descend.

INT. PARKING GARAGE
Hullen leads Lamb into a car. They drive off from the
building.

EXT. SUBURBAN STREET
Hullen pulls the car over. Lamb is sitting in the passenger seat.

HULLEN

Rudy, abandon John Lamb. Go back to who you
were and start over. It's not too late.

LAMB

I don't know what to say.

HULLEN

Just start over Rudy. Life isn't about being
judged by the size of your wallet. It's about the
size of your character.

LAMB

What about Judex?

HULLEN

I'll square it with him. You just straightened out
your life.

Lamb steps out of the car and Hullen drives off.

INT. FENCING ACADEMY DAYTIME

Both the Tremeuse brothers, Jack and Roger, are in fencing gear with their helmets under one arm as they grip
their swords. They smile at each other and place their
helmets on. Swords raised and in position, they begin.
This scene has various shots of the sword fight, with
both brothers feinting, scoring, jabbing and dueling.
There is an intensity to their ballet with blades.

INT. FAVRAUX MANSION - MORNING

Jacqueline is in the living room. She is at a desk, her
laptop on in front of her. There is much she must do.

With the attempt on her son, she knows that she could possibly be next. In the background, we hear a doorbell ring. Entering the room is the butler.

BUTLER
A Mr. Tremeuse is here to see you, Madam.

JACQUELINE
Send him in please.

Into the room walks Roger Tremeuse.

ROGER
Mrs. Aubrey, I hope I am not disturbing you.

JACQUELINE
You caught me by surprise. I was expecting to see your brother when I heard it was a Mr. Tremeuse.

ROGER
I actually get that more often than you would think. Especially from pretty ladies.

JACQUELINE
Is this a social call, or are you here on a visit from the District Attorney's office?

ROGER
Let's call it a little of both.

JACQUELINE
Would you like to sit?

ROGER

Thank you.

He sits in a chair near her.

ROGER (cont'd)
Can I start with a blunt question?

JACQUELINE
It runs in your family I see.

ROGER
Why didn't you report the kidnapping of your son?

JACQUELINE
How do you know about that?

ROGER
A tourist caught it on film. What happened?

JACQUELINE
I want to protect my son.

ROGER
You are aware that we found a dead body at the scene?

JACQUELINE
Yes.

ROGER

Are you also aware that we found the body of the other man that abducted your son in a hotel suite?

JACQUELINE
(shaken)
No...I wasn't. Why are you telling me this?

ROGER

I think you two know something about this Judex and I need to know what it is.

JACQUELINE

Your brother? What does he have to do with this?

ROGER

Something, nothing. I don't know. Can I tell you a story?

EXT. SUBURBAN STREET NIGHTTIME
Flashback. It is cold night out. The long black limo drives slowly from the suburbs. Inside is William Tremeuse and his wife, Ann. She is obviously pregnant as she is showing. The sleek vehicle turns a corner and a PREGNANT WOMAN staggers towards it, but falls before getting to the car. She is in pain.

ANN
Stop the car!

Mrs. Tremeuse climbs out of the car. Her husband follows her as she races to the woman. They get to her and Mrs. Tremeuse takes the woman in rags' hand.

>PREGNANT WOMAN
>My son... protect my son.

The woman of privilege looks into the eyes of the woman in rags and recognizes a kindred inner strength. When the woman covered in filth speaks, the love of the child within touches the other woman.

>PREGNANT WOMAN (cont'd)
>Do you have any children?

>ANN
>A son. He just isn't ready to come out.

>PREGNANT WOMAN
>Then you understand the love and protection a child needs. His father swore to kill his son...My son. Help me...please.

Ann Tremeuse looks into the pregnant woman's eyes. The women smile at each other.

>ANN
>We have to get you to the hospital.

>PREGNANT WOMAN
>No, no hospital.

>ANN
>What do you want us to do?

PREGNANT WOMAN

Help me deliver my son. I'm dying and he needs love that I won't be able to give him. Do you understand what I am asking?

ANN

Yes.

PREGNANT WOMAN

His father is coming and he must not find the boy. Keep my son. Raise him as yours with love. Can you?

The woman in the fur coat, takes it off to lay beneath the other woman in her car. Her husband helps to prop the woman's head on his suit jacket as he lays his hand on her shoulder.

WILLIAM TREMEUSE

We will.

In the city the alley cats sing a serenade as the cries of the baby greet the world he enters. We have a montage of birthing images.

ANN

Do you want to hold him?

PREGNANT WOMAN

Yes. But I can't. I won't let go if I do. Just love this boy.

The pregnant woman somehow staggers out of the limo into the night, never again to see her son.

Ann Tremeuse holds the baby boy and looks at her husband. She smiles as she kisses the boy's forehead. All of the sudden her expression changes. She has a strange look on her face.

                    WILLIAM TREMEUSE
Ann…

                    ANN
Oh my god. I'm going into labor.

INT. FAVRAUX MANSION
Roger Tremeuse has just finished telling Jacqueline Aubrey the story.

                    JACQUELINE
My God. I never heard that story.

                    ROGER
No one has. I haven't even told my fiancée, but for some reason I told you.

                    JACQUELINE
Did Jack ever meet his mother?

                    ROGER
Why do you assume it was Jack? Our parents told us the story but never told us which child was which. It never mattered to us. We're brothers that share the same passions and obsessions.

189

JACQUELINE

My father?

ROGER
(nodding his head)
He was one.

JACQUELINE

Thank you Roger. Thank you for sharing that
story with me.

ROGER

Good night Mrs. Aubrey. Be careful. There is
more going on and I don't think it is over yet.
I'll let myself out.

INT JUDEX SECRET HEADQUARTERS - MAIN
ROOM

Hullen is sitting at the monitors. Judex calls in. He is
visible on the monitor.

HULLEN

Judex, I have to speak to you.

JUDEX (V.O.)

Yes.

HULLEN

Lamb is gone...

JUDEX

Escaped?

HULLEN

No. I let him go.

JUDEX

Why? Why would you possibly let him go?

HULLEN

He was my son that I thought was dead.

JUDEX

Rudy? Lamb is Rudy?

A light goes off making Hullen turn. He sees Favraux on the floor, his body conditions dropping.

HULLEN

Favraux's down! Get here quickly!

INT. JUDEX SECRET HEADQUARTERS
FAVRAUX'S CELL

Hullen comes in and sees Favraux on the ground. As he rolls him over, Favraux wrestles with him. This is a death fight, two men who hate each other. Hullen throws Favraux to the far side, then moves in for the kill, but, suddenly, he stops and grabs his chest. He looks at Favraux in shock... then drops to the ground. Favraux looks down at Hullen, kicks the body and leaves the cell.

INT. JUDEX SECRET HEADQUARTERS
CELLBLOCK HALLWAY

Favraux is walking quickly down the cellblock. He hears the cries all about him from those that he feels betrayed him. He has one goal in his mind. Escape. But, they betrayed him. He turns back to face the music.

<u>EXT. CITY STREET.</u>
Coming out of a doorway in a city alleyway is Favraux.
He looks up and recognizes his building. It is the first
time he has seen light in some time. The brightness of it
hurts his eyes, but he doesn't care. He is free. He walks
along the street enjoying every smell.

<u>INT. MONTI & MORALES APARTMENT EARLY
EVENING</u>
They are inside the apartment. Both appear getting ready
to go, they look sexy as hell. There is a knock at the
door. Monti grabs a pistol while Morales opens the door.
Standing in the doorway, looking tired and hungry but
still noble and in control is Favraux.

FAVRAUX
My Valkyries.

<u>INT. JUDEX SECRET HEADQUARTERS</u>
Hullen is laying on the ground, holding onto life until
Judex arrives.

HULLEN
(Coughing)

JUDEX
Don't talk. I'll get help.

HULLEN
You must stop Favraux. Promise me. Promise
me.

JUDEX

I promise.

Hullen coughs again and then closes his eyes, giving up his ghost.

INT. APARTMENT OF MONTI AND MORALES

Favraux is sitting at a table with a bottle of absinthe before him and a steaming plate of food. He is showered and dressed and all business. He then prepares the Absinthe.

FAVRAUX

That is better. Now I feel like talking.

MONTI

We saw you die.

FAVRAUX

You saw what Judex wanted you to see.

MORALES

How did you escape?

FAVRAUX

Because my desire to live was stronger than his desire to incarcerate me. How is my organization?

MORALES

It had fallen apart. We rescued it.

MONTI

We control it, baby. It is all yours.

MORALES
Lamb and Cocantin did leave the ranch though.
They kidnapped your grandson.

FAVRAUX
So I was told. My daughter, she is well?

MONTI
She is giving away your estate to charity.

FAVRAUX
Let her. To the world, I am dead.

MONTI
But your fortune, baby...

FAVRAUX
...Exists off shore in many dummy companies
and identities. For every dollar the world
thought I had, I had five hidden. Now, we have
much to do. I want Judex.

INT HOME - COCANTIN
Cocantin is in her home. The doorbell rings. She takes
out her gun and walks to it.

COCANTIN
Yes...

LAMB (O.S.)
Open up Jenny... It's John.

Cocantin opens the door for Lamb to enter. He stops and looks at her hard. He has choices to make.

COCANTIN
Where have you been! I thought Judex had you.

LAMB
Get me a drink. He did.

COCANTIN
How did you get away?

LAMB
Forget about that. He has Favraux. He's alive.

INT.   JUDEX   SECRET   HEADQUARTERS
CELLBLOCK- AFTERNOON
Judex enters the building as he wants to check on the prisoners, but, lo and behold, each cell is closed, but the people within the cells all lie dead, shot to death. He is upset, getting madder and madder with each passing step. We watch him speed walk from cell to cell, the same thing at each one. Until we get to the last cell. The camera enters with Judex. Hanging from the door of what was Favraux's cell is a note. We come over Judex's shoulder to read it.

FAVRAUX (V.O.)
My dear Judex. We have unfinished business. My country estate. Tonight. Favraux.

EXT. WOODS - DUSK
Side of a road. A SUV pulls up in a secluded area. A figure in the shadows steps out. He looks around, confi-

dent that the car is where it can't be seen and he walks around to the back. Opening the trunk, he starts to transform himself into the figure in black, Judex. And as Judex he heads off into the woods.

INT. FAVRAUX MANSION
Jacqueline is walking through the house. Her butler approaches, quicker than normal, almost urgent.

> BUTLER
> We have a problem.

Jacqueline walks to a window to look out. The yard is filled with the Rastafarians, lead by Foreman. They are armed and up to no good. The butler reaches for a phone to call the police.

> BUTLER (cont'd)
> The line is dead.

Jacqueline takes out her cell phone, and dials. The phone rings and rings.

> JACQUELINE
> Come on, pick up...

The door opens abruptly and the Rastafarians enter the home. The butler jumps between Aubrey and the men, but he is shot down, while Aubrey screams.

Foreman walks over to her, and takes her by the arm, not very gently. The front door then opens and Lamb and Cocantin enter. Aubrey struggles to no avail. Lamb has never been more confident in his entire life.

<u>INT. FAVRAUX'S SUMMER ESTATE</u>
Favraux is there with his two women companions, Monti and Morales. It is command center central. Also at the compound are Giordanio and Zhou.

> MONTI
> Baby, we have Giordanio's men on the outer pe-rimeter and Zhou's on the inside.

> MORALES
> No one is getting in here without us knowing.

> FAVRAUX
> Where is Holland?

> MONTI
> He offered to serve as the back up.

Favraux places a cigar in his mouth. He lights it. Turning to Giordanio he looks him in the eyes.

> FAVRAUX
> You have failed me in the past, Giordanio. Your men guarded me when Judex came in and took me. Do not fail me again.

> GIORDANIO
> I don't know what happened and how the Hell you came back from the dead, but it wasn't my fault.

> FAVRAUX
> Be sure of the results this time.

Favraux turns to Zhou. He looks at her.

> FAVRAUX (cont'd)
> My Valkyries will stay with me, my pet, but I
> depend on you to be where they can't. No one
> gets past you.

> ZHOU
> No one. Judex likes to play with swords, we will
> teach him how to play with swords.

Zhou walks to leave.

> FAVRAUX
> Then let Judex come to us.

FOREST DUSK
Two men with machine guns walk through the forest,
looking both ways. They have walkie talkies hooked into
their ears as they go by.

We see Judex line up the arrow in the bow and his fingers release the arrow. The furthest away guard turns
and falls, an arrow sticking out of him. The other guard
turns and falls also with an arrow in his chest. Judex runs
off.

FAVRAUX'S SUMMER ESTATE DUSK
Favraux is waiting with his female guards near him.
Zhou is close by and Giordanio is standing close, having
a drink. The phone rings. Giordanio answers it.

GIORDANIO
Favraux, you have a call.

Favraux walks over. He looks at Giordanio and his utter
lack of respect.

FAVRAUX
Who is on the line?

GIORDANIO
Let me put them on speaker.

Giordanio places the receiver in a cradle and pushes a
button.

GIORDANIO (cont'd)
Okay, you have the fatman's attention. Speak.

LAMB (O.S.)
Fatman. You should have stayed dead.

FAVRAUX
You have balls, Lamb, to speak to me like that.

LAMB (O.S.)
I have more than balls, I have your daughter.

FAVRAUX
You dare to touch her?

COCANTIN (O.S.)
We dare to kill the bitch if you don't do what we
tell you.

FAVRAUX
Feeling brave detective? What do you want?

LAMB (O.S.)
Your money, what else would we want from you. Giordanio?

GIORDANIO
Yeah?

COCANTIN (O.S.)
Bring him to us. And kill the bitches.

The Line goes dead.

Giordanio has a gun out and trained on Favraux that was not seen before. He turns it to Monti and Morales and tightens his finger on the trigger.

In a flash, Zhou has a dart out and throws it, embedding in Giordanio's hand. He screams in pain. Zhou has a knife in her hand and slashes up and down on Giordanio.

FAVRAUX
Traitor. Where is my daughter?

GIORDANIO
Go to Hell.

Giordanio spits blood out at Favraux's feet. That is the wrong answer. Favraux nods at Zhou who kneels down and uses the knife in ways that are best not seen, but the cries and screams from Giordanio let us know that the pain is enormous.

GIORDANIO (cont'd)
Okay, okay, Jesus Christ, don't kill me. I'll tell
you. They have her at your warehouse...please
man, don't kill me.

FAVRAUX
I won't kill you...

Both Monti and Morales take out their guns and empty
their clips in him.

FAVRAUX (cont'd)
My pet, you stay here. When Judex comes, kill
him. We will await you at my home after I finish
with my traitors.

ZHOU
(She nods her head)

THE FOREST - DUSK
The camera in a montage of shots shows the viewer that
there are many bodies that lay cold and dead on the
ground, all with arrows in them.

Judex in the last shot can be seen stalking through the
woods, his sword out, the bow tossed aside on the
ground.

Reverse shot from before. In front of the main house, we
have five members of Zhou's group. They are waiting,
as if they know that Judex is coming.

He steps out before them, his sword on display. They respond with their swords out. Above on a balcony, is Zhou watching the display below.

The first warrior charges Judex, who fends him off with his sword and in a reverse move, a Swish Slash Swash move, slices across his stomach, killing him as his intestines fall to the ground. The second and third warriors attack together, but Judex side steps one and blocks the blows of the other as he goes on the offensive. While dealing with second and third, the fourth enters the fray, not waiting for his companions to finish. Like Itto Ogami in *Lone Wolf and Cub*, Judex moves his sword at lightning speed, killing the three remaining men. They stand, dead on their feet for a moment, then as Judex turns to face the fifth warrior, they fall over dead.

Judex and the final warrior size each other up. He has seen him in action and knows that Judex has skill with the blade. They each prepare and strike a pose waiting for the battle to begin. Above from the balcony, Zhou watches, and then, from the body language, she knows something that the audience does not. It is time for her to join Favraux. She turns and leaves.

The final warrior and Judex hold their positions like marble statues in the moonlight. Finally, the warrior moves. His blade sings in the night as it swoops down for Judex. Judex responds as his blade then swings forward. Both warriors hold the next, post swing position. Neither moves. Finally Zhou's warrior falls over dead.

Judex moves on to the main house.

INT. FAVRAUX SUMMER HOME

Judex enters into the house, his sword away. The time for stealth and quiet are gone. Both pistols are in his hands as he makes his way through the mansion. The emptiness is reflected in the silence. The ringing of a telephone breaks the quiet.

> TELEPHONE ANSWERING MACHINE
> Please leave a message at the beep.
> (Favraux's voice through machine)
> Judex, if you hear this, it means that you have defeated my warm up guests for you. I did mean to be there, but unfortunately, my daughter has been taken prisoner by two of my former aids, Lamb and Cocantin. I am en-route to my warehouse on Front Street. Telling you serves two purposes. First, should they capture me, it will be up to you to free me so you can take me back to your loving care. Second, it provides me with the back up I need walking into the lion's den. What do you say?

Judex picks up the phone to speak into the receiver.

> JUDEX
> I'll be there.

INT. POLICE STATION - NIGHT

Kinahan is sitting at his desk. There is a visitor. It is Roger Tremeuse. Kinahan nods to him.

They walk to the rear of the building into an office that is empty.

KINAHAN

You're slumming Roger. What brings you my way?

ROGER

Killing time I guess.

KINAHAN

It's this Judex, isn't it? I can't clear my desk because of the crap involved.

Roger Tremeuse's cell phone rings.

ROGER

Hello?

JUDEX (O.S.)

Assistant District Attorney Tremeuse?

ROGER

Yes...

JUDEX (O.S.)

This is Judex. Listen carefully. Richard Favraux is alive. His daughter has been kidnapped.

ROGER

Where is she?

JUDEX (O.S.)

You don't listen very well, counselor. I will call you so be ready for my call.

ROGER

Who are you Judex? Why are you telling me
this?

JUDEX (O.S.)

Be ready for my call.

WAREHOUSE - EXT NIGHT

Favraux pulls up in his limousine. He gets out and walks
toward the entrance.

WAREHOUSE INT. NIGHT LOBBY

Favraux walks into the lobby area. Three armed Rastafarians come down to greet him. Favraux opens his coat
and turns around slowly to show them what he carrying.

FAVRAUX

I am unarmed and alone. Where is my daughter?

Holland and Foreman walk into view at this moment.
They are on an upper landing looking down at the large
man.

HOLLAND

Bring the fatman up.

One of the Rastafarians pokes Favraux with his gun as
they walk over to the stairwell.

WAREHOUSE INT MAIN OFFICE

Favraux is ushered into an office. Sitting in a chair is
Holland. He obviously sees himself as the big cheese.
Beside him on a desk is Foreman. Both appear confi-
dent. They believe that they have an upper hand on

Favraux at this juncture. A chair is pulled out for Favraux by one of the henchmen. Favraux takes it and looks relaxed as he sits.

FAVRAUX
You invited me, and I am here.

HOLLAND
You don't look so big now, fatman.

FAVRAUX
Are we going to spend all night talking about my weight, or get to why you invited me? I want to see my daughter.

FOREMAN
We tell you what is what. Not you no more. When you died, you lost your power.

FAVRAUX
Then what do you want with me?

HOLLAND
Money. Like I told you before. We want your money.

Favraux reaches into his pockets and pulls out a roll. He starts to peel off bills, dropping them to the floor in front of him.

FAVRAUX
Well, they didn't bury me with a lot of cash, so I don't have much on me.

HOLLAND
Don't you try to play us.

FAVRAUX
Who, me play you? Two smart operators like yourselves? All I want is my daughter. And where are your "leaders?"

HOLLAND
Hell, they work with us, not us for them.

FAVRAUX
I doubt they see it that way.

Holland gets out of his chair and walks about the room.

HOLLAND
We need to talk about the money.

FAVRAUX
When I "died," my money went to Jacqueline. From what I understand, she has begun donating all of it to charity.

Entering into the room are Lamb and Cocantin. They are smug.

LAMB
And I know you Favraux. You are too damn smart to not have funds in other places that no one would know about. That's what we want.

FAVRAUX
How much do you want?

LAMB

I don't want to be greedy. Let's say a hundred million. Each.

FAVRAUX

And that will be the end of it? No more trips to the well, kidnapping members of my family every time you have a car payment due?

LAMB

You have my word.

FAVRAUX

That doesn't mean much to me.

LAMB

You're calling me a liar?

FAVRAUX

That's mild to what I would say. For a thief and a murderer and now a kidnapper, you are sensitive.

FOREMAN

Wasn't Giordanio supposed to bring him?

COCANTIN

Where is Giordanio?

FAVRAUX

He's dead. I don't take betrayal well.

The four gangsters look about the room. They all have had the same thought, that if Giordanio is dead and Favraux came under his own accord, then they will have Monti and Morales to deal with. And possibly Zhou.

                    COCANTIN
        Get more men downstairs, quick!

Foreman runs out of the room with his gun out as he shouts instructions to the men. Favraux stays calm in the seat.

                    FAVRAUX
        What's wrong? I came as you requested.

                    HOLLAND
        Where are those crazy bitches of yours? Jesus
        Christ, Giordanio was supposes to take care of
        this!

From behind Holland, a figure in black appears out of nowhere. He dives forward, knocking him to the ground. It is Judex. He is on top of Holland and has an automatic weapon out aimed at Favraux. The people in the room scatter.

                    JUDEX
        Hold it there Favraux.
                (Turning to Holland)
        Where's his daughter?

                    HOLLAND
        Here, she's here.

JUDEX
Take me to her.

Holland is slowly let up by Judex. He leads Favraux and
Judex down the corridor. In the distance we hear gunfire
and see smoke.

WAREHOUSE INT. MAIN FOYER
In a cut away shot, Monti and Morales have just arrived
and there is Hell to pay. They are armed to the teeth and
blasting like two angels of death at everyone in their
way.

WAREHOUSE INT. HALLWAY
Holland guides Judex and Favraux to a room. He stops
in front of the door.

HOLLAND
In there.

JUDEX
Alone?

HOLLAND
Yeah, man, she is alone.

JUDEX
(turning to Favraux)
He's yours to watch. I will get your daughter.

Judex burst into the room.

WAREHOUSE INT DIMLY LIT ROOM

On an unmade bed is Jacqueline Aubrey. She is bound and gagged. Sitting in two chairs are the guards.

The door burst open and Judex flies in. He rolls on the ground as the first guard fires a burst at him. Judex fires once, hitting the man in the chest as the second man fires wildly at him. Judex rolls away from where Jacqueline is laying, and fires at the man forcing him to dive for cover, to where Judex dives also and he comes up with the pistol aimed directly between the man's eyes. The explosion rocks the room as Judex's gun goes off.

Judex moves to the bed where Jacqueline lies. She recoils in horror and fear, not sure of what Judex means to her. He takes a sharp blade out and cuts her ties.

JUDEX

You're safe now.

JACQUELINE

Why do you keep helping me? You killed my father.

JUDEX

Brace yourself, Jacqueline.

Jacqueline looks in shock at Judex. Favraux enters the room with Holland.

Jacqueline races over to her father. They embrace and his eyes close in joy. He thought he would never see her again because of his incarceration and she because of his being dead.

JUDEX (cont'd)

There is a war going on downstairs. We have to
move.

FAVRAUX

What about him?

JUDEX

Leave him. There has been too much bloodshed.

Favraux fires a pistol at Holland, killing him. Jacqueline
screams.

FAVRAUX

Another drop in the bucket.

WARE HOUSE INT. HALLWAY.

The three leave the room. The sounds of the gunfight are
getting louder, then they abruptly stop. Standing before
Judex, Favraux and Jacqueline are Monti and Morales.

MONTI

Let them go, Judex.

JUDEX

I can't do that.

The two women look at each other, smile, then rush in
attack toward Judex. As they rush forward, Favraux
pushes Jacqueline forward with him out the way of the
battle.

Judex stands ready, waiting for the attack then moves in a counter attack toward them. A side kick from Monti narrowly misses Judex's head, while Morales fires at Judex. A punch from Morales connects with his side. The two women are a raging dynamo, attacking Judex in perfect rhythm.

At the same time, Favraux pulls his daughter by her hand, leading her towards an exit of the building.

The fight with the two tigresses rages on. Judex finally stops blocking their attacks and goes on the offensive. In a fast series of moves, he sends Morales flying backwards as a new hail of bullets enters the scene. Morales and Monti's faces rage in anger as their attention is pulled upon by the rushing in police, causing them to look at each other, then Judex. Both smile at him, then turn and race out into the night, pursued from below by the men in blue.

Judex, hidden from the rain of bullets, stands exhausted as the police leave to chase Monti and Morales. He turns and prepares to go after Favraux when, before him, in all her radiant beauty, is Zhou. Her sword is out and she signals Judex to come forward. He takes out his sword and the two run forward at each other, swords over their heads, to end in a fast series of blows. Judex overtakes Zhou and with a final swing, takes her head.

VOICE

Freeze!

213

From below, the room is filled with two policemen, Kinahan and Roger Tremeuse. Judex does not freeze and takes off running as bullets whiz by behind him.

Judex turns and is face to face with Cocantin. She fires at him, and he throws his sword toward her, killing her.

Judex begins running again. He spots Lamb with Foreman, guns out. He dives through the air and comes up on Foreman first, his blade slashing through his arm, then up gutting him.

Judex is before Lamb, both with weapons out.

                    JUDEX
          Rudy, it doesn't have to be this way.

                    LAMB
          There is no other way.

                    JUDEX
          Your father is dead.

                    LAMB
          He died to me a long time ago.

Lamb fires his weapon at Judex as Roger and Kinahan turn the corner, firing at the pair. Judex takes off running away, as Lamb enters into a fire fight, dying there on the spot.

As Judex runs, searching for Favraux and Jacqueline, a pipe lands on his head, knocking the helmet and mask away, but we don't see his face yet.

Favraux stands above him, wielding the pipe. The un-masked Judex looks up. Jacqueline recoils in a second shock.

FAVRAUX

Tremeuse?

JACQUELINE

Jack?

Judex rises, taking advantage of the momentary stillness. Favraux recovers his senses and swings the pipe again at Judex, who ducks, and swings back.

The two men fight hand to hand with Judex finally gaining what looks like the upper hand. He is above Favraux about to deal a death blow. Jacqueline grabs a gun off the ground and has it aimed at Judex.

JACQUELINE (cont'd)

STOP!

JUDEX

Jacqueline...You don't understand. He killed my father.

JACQUELINE
(crying)
So you are going to kill my father? An eye for an eye?

The door burst open. It is Roger Tremeuse with his gun out. He sees a room of confusion. His brother in the

Judex uniform; Favraux alive and on the ground; and Jacqueline Aubrey with a gun out.

ROGER
Jacqueline...put the gun down... Please.

Jacqueline is confused. She has not dropped the gun. Her dead father is alive. The man that she has counted on is the masked avenger that she thought killed her father, yet rescued her son.

Favraux springs up in a burst of strength out of Judex grip, grabbing a gun off the ground, firing at Roger.

Roger fires his weapon twice as Judex knocks the gun out of Jacqueline's hand. Falling on the ground from the gunshots of Roger is Favraux. Jacqueline drops to the ground to her father.

Roger looks at his brother. Jack picks up his mask. He looks at Jacqueline and then Roger.

JACQUELINE
Daddy...

FAVRAUX
Jacqueline...I have more sins than you have the prayers to ask for forgiveness.

JACQUELINE
Hold on Daddy...Daddy?

Favraux closes his eyes.

ROGER

Get out of here.

Judex turns and leaves the room.

Roger and Jacqueline just look at each other.

LAS VEGAS – NIGHT - THE CITY
Exterior shot that shows the grandeur of the city. The camera shows various buildings from a variety of shots, but it slowly focuses on a very old building, going slowly in.

LAS VEGAS NIGHT INTERIOR BUILDING
Long, dark hallways are in this lower section of the building. Men in uniforms, unlike anything we have ever seen, with an insignia that has never been seen by the world, stand guard. The camera passes all of this to go to a doorway that two men stand guard before.

INTERIOR BUILDING NIGHT CONFERENCE ROOM
About a table, nine powerful men and women sit. They are seen in the shadows. All we see clearly is their hands on the table. They each wear a ring that also bears the insignia that we saw on the guards.

At the head of the table, dressed in black is the leader. Before him is a crystal goblet filled with a thick red wine. A man of power that has led others for longer than any can recall, yet he is as young and powerful appearing as he was years before. His name is LORD RUTHVEN.

MAN #1

Our businesses report in well. Communications is up 14% from last quarter, entertainment up 25% and energy seeing the greatest increases almost 83%. Pharmaceutical rose parallel to narcotics, which is interesting as never before have our light and dark been equal.

MAN #2

The wars serve us well. People need entertainment, news and escape. Reward the presidents, they followed their instructions well.

MAN #1

We have Favraux's seat at the council to fill. He was almost a candidate for joining the inner circle.

WOMAN #2

And it has been twenty years since Tremeuse killed himself. His seat is still vacant. The Tremeuse family has had a seat at our council for six hundred years.

MAN #1

His son has grown his arms business to rival some of ours. Perhaps him?

RUTHVEN

Perhaps. He knows nothing of our activities, but he bears watching. Now, what is the report?

WOMAN #1

It has begun. The stars have neared the formation and the planets are entering the alignment for the final confrontation.

MAN #1

And the thousandth one has awakened.

RUTHVEN

He is the last?

MAN #1

There can be only one that is born into his role in destiny.

RUTHVEN

Then how do we know he is reborn?

WOMAN #2
    (in an old voice with old withered
    hands)

Because I have seen it. He has awakened and the call is beating in his chest. He just does not understand what the calling is. He is confused.

RUTHVEN

Will he answer the call?

WOMAN #1

It is his destiny.

RUTHVEN

Have they found him yet?

WOMAN #2
They seek him also.

RUTHVEN
Where is the beast?

WOMAN #1
We have the beast. He is awaiting his final trans-
formation.

MAN # 1
Then he will kill the Last One?

WOMAN #2
No, he will prepare the way for he who will.

RUTHVEN
And who is that?

WOMAN #2
His son.

RUTHVEN
Then it has begun.

WOMAN #2
Not until he kills you also.

INT JACK TREMEUSE OFFICE MORNING
Jack is behind his desk. His phone rings.

SUSAN (O.S.)
Your mother and brother are here.

JACK

Send them in please.

His brother Roger and Ann Tremeuse walk in through the office door. Jack rises and walks to his family. His mother embraces him.

ANN

It's over.

JACK

It will never be over. A line was crossed and...

ROGER

Jack, it's over.

ANN

I'll let you two talk. I love you both, and you love each other, so you'll find a way to work this out.

Ann walks out.

ROGER

Hey.

JACK

You here to arrest me?

ROGER

No. I'm shocked I wasn't arrested either. She didn't press charges against either of us.

JACK

How do I tell her how I feel about her, after keeping her father as my prisoner?

ROGER

You want to talk about this?

JACK

It's really over then. Isn't it?

ROGER

We have a few unexplainable dead bodies, starting with Favraux. We fixed it up. He's dead, let him stay dead. Then there is your alter ego, Judex.

JACK

There's Judex.

ROGER

Is he retired?

JACK

Favraux's gone, but there are innocent people that Justice abandoned. They need Judex.

ROGER

That's going to be a problem for the next DA. Guess I should run then.

JACK

Guess you should. How is Jacqueline? She's been through a lot.

ROGER

She didn't say anything about you being Judex.
My shot killed her father and she still said nothing except to let the world think he was always
dead. Why, I don't know.

JACK

I don't know what to say to her. What do you
and I say to each other? I planned my life, my
whole life for revenge on that bastard.

ROGER

And I killed him. Mister follow the book, and
what do I do? Shoot him.

JACK

No court would ever...

ROGER

I know the courts. I know the law. I also know
how I feel.

JACK

How?

ROGER

Not like I thought. No remorse. No guilt. Almost...relief that he is dead. And pleasure that I
killed him. For Pop. For Mom. Hell, mainly for
me.

JACK

Roger...

ROGER

Save it Jack... Favraux's dead. Pop can rest now.

JACK

Sure you're okay?

ROGER

Yeah...I'm good. You?

JACK

I'm good. It's over.

Roger and Jack Tremeuse hug.

FAVRAUX MANSION MORNING BACK YARD

Jacqueline is walking on the grounds. Jack walks up to her. Slow steady shot leading up to her as he walks towards her.

JACQUELINE

Hello Jack.

JACK

Hello Jacqueline.

There is a strong awkward moment of silence between them. They have a strained laugh because of it, but the fact is that neither knows what to say.

JACK (cont'd)

Jacqueline...

JACQUELINE

Are you going to make excuses? Try to explain what happened? That you, a man I came to trust, was Judex?

JACK

I don't know where to begin.

JACQUELINE

There is nowhere. I lost my father... twice. You can't replace that or fix the hurt that I had. I have him back now. He is where he can't be hurt anymore.

JACK

What do you mean...Roger's shot killed him.

JACQUELINE

No Jack. He's alive. I'm telling you because if anything ever happens to him again, I'll know it was you.

JACK

It's over Jacqueline. Your father is safe, I swear it, and will protect him.

JACQUELINE

How will you protect him?

JACK

You will have to trust me, but I will. No one will know he lives. No one. I blamed your father for what happened to my father, and you have every reason to hate me for what happened with your father.

JACQUELINE

I don't hate you. I don't know how I feel. But I don't hate you.

JACK

But justice has to be served. Sometimes it goes beyond the law. That is the role that Judex serves.

JACQUELINE

I don't know if I can accept that. Is the role of a vigilante acceptable Jack? What if our roles were reversed?

JACK

They were. And I did what I did. For hurting you, I'm sorry.

JACQUELINE

I'm sure you are. Jack, I need time to get my life back in order. To be with Charlie.

JACK

What happens to you? What happens to us?

JACQUELINE

Me. My father needs my help and I need his as I will focus on the charity. Making sure the money gets to where it is suppose to go. As for us, there is no us. At least not now. I have a lot to sort out, Jack.

                    JACK
I understand.

                  JACQUELINE
I hope you do Jack. I really hope you do. How
about you? Is Judex retired?

<u>EXT. NIGHT IN PHILADELPHIA.</u>
Judex is standing with a blue moon behind him. The
camera zooms in on him.

                  JUDEX (V.O.)
As long as innocent people are hurt Judex will
be there.

                                        FADE OUT.

ABOUT THE AUTHOR

Robert L. ROBINSON, Jr. is the Founder, President, Chief Imagination Officer and creative vision of Arupt Entertainment as well as the Co-President of Framelight Productions. Arupt Entertainment is developing transmedia projects for diverse media platforms while Framelight Productions options comic books and novels for projects in Hollywood including *Deadworld, Sword of Wood, Dr. Deth with Kip and Muffy, Slackergirl,* and others and partners with producers such as Bill Mechanic, David Hayter, Scott Mednick, Larry Hama and others. Robinson is a life-long entrepreneur with a passion for both film and comic books. With this combined passion came the screenplay *Judex*. Robinson has been married since 1988 and has 4 children ages 22-11. He is a resident of Drexel Hill, PA.